Y0-BQY-118

# ROBERT SILVERBERG
By the award-winning author of *STAR OF THE GYPSIES*.

# TIME OF THE GREAT FREEZE

A TOM DOHERTY ASSOCIATES BOOK

TIME OF THE GREAT FREEZE

Copyright © 1964 by Robert Silverberg; Introduction copyright © 1980 by Robert Silverberg

First Tor Printing: February 1988

A TOR Book

Published by Tom Doherty Associates, Inc.
49 West 24th Street
New York, NY 10010

ISBN: 0-812-55469-8
Can. No.: 0-812-55470-1

Printed in the United States of America

0  9  8  7  6  5  4  3  2  1

In 2200 the world began to grow cold.

Ice accummulated, hundreds of feet thick across the top of the world, and as the weight increased, the ice began to flow. Glaciers—rivers of ice—crept southward.

"The winters are getting colder," people said, but it was twenty years before anyone realized that a major trend was under way. Each year the mean temperature was a fraction of a degree lower than it had been the year before. Some villages of Alaska, Canada, and Sweden had to be evacuated as the glaciers crept down toward them.

By 2230 everyone knew what was happening, and why. The sun and all its planets, it was found, as they moved together through the universe had been engulfed by a vast cloud of cosmic debris, and an all but infinite number of dust motes were screening and blocking the sun's radiation from Earth. To the eye everything still looked the same; the sky was just as blue, the clouds as fleecy. The cosmic dust could not be seen, but its effect could be felt. Invisible, it shrouded the sun, cut off the golden warmth. And so immense was the cloud that it would take centuries for the Solar System to pass entirely through it!

A new Ice Age began, and man retreated to cities far below the hostile surface, to await the return of warmth.

Look for these Tor books by Robert Silverberg

*To Everett Orr*

# Contents

# Introduction

I used to live in New York, a place where snow has been known occasionally to fall. I had a fine grand house up in the northern reaches of the city, close to the Westchester County line. That fine grand house had a fine grand driveway and a fine grand front walk, and every time we got a fine grand snowstorm I came out with my shovel and set to work. It was good exercise, and no doubt the quantities of snow I shoveled in the early 1960s do much to explain the generally good health I enjoy here in the late 1970s—but somewhere between then and now I decided I had had enough of that kind of exercise, and I moved to California. Out here a little snow sometimes falls, seven or eight times in a century, and the inhabitants assemble in the streets and stare at it in wonder and reverence and, if there is enough of it, gather it up to make snowballs, which they lob ineptly at one another amid great giggles. At least, that's how it was the last time it snowed in my part of California, and I may live long enough to see it happen again, though I'm in no hurry for it. Snow may be a charming novelty to native Californians, but it's one of the things I came out here to get away from.

The winter of 1962-63 was a notably snowy one in New York. I wielded the shovel constantly, and there were times when I had just barely finished hacking a path to the street when the sky turned that ominous iron-gray color and a new load of the stuff came down. I recall a period of seven or eight weeks in a row when there was a major snowstorm every Saturday night, so that I would awaken to a world of whiteness on Sunday morning and have to go out and excavate a thirty-foot swathe in order to find the copy of the *New York Times* that was supposed to provide me with amusement by the fireside on Sunday mornings.

All that snow was very much on my mind in the spring of 1963 when I proposed doing a science fiction novel for the young readers' division of Holt, Rinehart & Winston. *Time of the Great Freeze*, I called it: a novel of the next ice age. I was already doing research for a non-fiction book on Antarctica, *The Loneliest Continent*, and my studies on the world of prehistoric man had given me some familiarity with Pleistocene conditions, so it was no difficult matter for me to postulate a world of the near future in which minor climatic adjustments had sent glaciers marching once more over the world. The winter I had just endured had left me convinced, well into March or perhaps early April, that glaciers would any day now come sliding down out of White Plains or Yonkers and come to rest in my driveway.

I signed the contract for *Time of the Great Freeze* in May of 1963 and began to write the book in July. It does not snow in New York in July. The summer weather in New York, in truth, is something other than polar. There I sat, day after day, in 95° weather and 950% humidity, slaving over my typewriter while the air-conditioner struggled wearily to cope, and I wrote of bitter cold, I wrote of knife-sharp winds, I wrote of fields of ice so bright they stung the eye, so frosty they burned the skin. It was a heroic act of the imagination. Each morning, settling in at my desk, I closed my eyes, I journeyed backward in memory some six months, I saw myself grimly setting forth in boots and parka, shovel in hand, to excavate my Sunday *Times*, and gradually I started to shiver, I felt my nose and cheeks turn brittle, I huddled in against the cruel wintry blasts, and I began to write. . . . and after a few sweaty hours staggered downstairs to dunk myself in the swimming pool. And so it went. There in the tropical heat of the New York summer I visualized a frozen Earth, and transmitted my vision to paper, and finally brought my valiant band of adventurers safely through to a land of mild weather and fleecy skies, and never once did I think of abandoning New York myself for some place where the climate was favorable to human habitation.

Years later I joined the great westward migration and ended up just across the bay from San Francisco, in a place where fuchsias and camelias are blooming merrily on this sunny February day, where the winters never get very cold and the summers never get very warm, a never-never-land of gentle breezes, and I think kind sad thoughts about my poor old mother and the eight million others who nobly endure the rigors of life back east, sacrificing themselves rather than adding to the population problems of our happy, if somewhat geologically unstable, land. And for all of them, and all of you, here is *Time of the Great Freeze* in print again. It was, long ago, a selection of the Junior Literary Guild, and in its hardcover edition received all sorts of flattering reviews which I would quote if I knew where I had filed them, and in its earlier paperback edition it sold quite well and went into several printings, and, all things considered, I suppose it was usefully inspirational for me to have had to do all that snow-shoveling in the winter of 1962-63. On the other hand, I'd rather live in California.

—Robert Silverberg
Oakland, California
February 1978

# TIME OF THE GREAT FREEZE

## City Under the Ice

IT WAS LATE IN THE DAY—OR WHAT PASSED FOR DAY IN the underground city of New York. Pale lights glimmered in the corridors of Level C. Figures moved quietly down the long hallway. At this hour, most New Yorkers were settling down for a quiet, restful evening.

Jim Barnes paused in front of a sturdy door in the residential section of Level C, and rapped smartly with his knuckles. He waited a moment, running his hand tensely through his thick shock of bright red hair. The door opened, after a long moment, and a short, blocky figure appeared. It was Ted Callison, whose room this was.

"Jim. Come on in. We've already made contact."

"I got here as soon as I could," Jim said. "Is my father here yet?"

"Ten minutes ago. Everyone's here. We've got London on the wireless."

Jim stepped into the room. Callison closed the door behind him and dogged it shut. Jim stood there a moment, a tall, rangy boy of seventeen, deceptively slender, for he was stronger than he looked.

Half a dozen faces confronted the newcomer. Jim knew them all well. His father, Dr. Raymond Barnes, was there. Chunky Ted Callison, capable in his field of electronics. Nimble-witted, blue-eyed Roy Veeder, one of the city's cleverest lawyers. Dom Hannon, small and wiry, whose specialty was the study of languages, philology. Brawny, muscular Chet Farrington, he of the legendary appetite, a zoologist by profession. And Dave Ellis, plump and short, a meterologist, who studied the changing weather of the world far above the city.

Six men. Jim, who was studying to be a hydroponics engineer, learning how to grow plants without soil or sun, was the seventh. Jim's heart pounded. What these men were doing was illegal, almost blasphemous—and he was one of them, he was part of the group, he shared the risk as an equal partner.

For six months now they had been meeting here in Ted Callison's room. At first, their goal had seemed hopeless, a wild dream. But the months had passed, and through long nights of toil they had put the radio equipment back into working order after decades on the shelf, and now . . .

"Speak up, New York!" a tinny voice cried out of nowhere. "We can barely hear you! Speak up, I say!"

"It's London," Roy Veeder murmured to Jim.

London! At last—contact with another city!

Like a priest before some strange idol Ted Callison crouched by the table and feverishly adjusted dials. Callison, whose broad face and ruddy light-brown skin told of his American Indian descent, was probably the best electronics technician in New York—which wasn't really saying too much. It was he who had restored the set to working order. Now he desperately manipulated the controls, trying to screen out interference.

Dr. Barnes grasped the microphone so tightly his knuckles whitened, and he leaned forward to speak. A historian by profession and something of a rebel by temperament, he was as thin as his son, but an astonishingly deep voice rumbled out of him: "London, this is New York calling. Do you hear us better now? Do you hear us?"

"We hear you, New York. Your accent is hard to understand, but we hear you!"

"This is Raymond Barnes, London. Barnes. I spoke last week with a Thomas Whitcomb."

A pause. Then:

"He is dead, Raymond Barnes," came London's answer, the words clipped and almost incomprehensible.

"Dead?"

"He died yesterday. It was by mischance —accident. He was found by . . ." The signal faded out, buried by noise. Callison toiled frenziedly with his controls. ". . . am Noel Hunt, his

3

cousin," came a blurp of sound unexpectedly. "What do you want, New York?"

"Why—to talk!" Dr. Barnes said in surprise. "It's hundreds of years since the last contact between London and New York!"

". . . did not hear you . . ."

"Hundred of years since the last contact! No record of contact since twenty-three hundred!"

"We have tried to reach you by wireless," the Londoner said. "There has never been any response."

"Now there is! Listen to me, Noel Hunt. We think the ice is retreating! We think it's time for man to come up out of these caves! Do you hear what I say, London?"

"I hear you, New York." The London voice sounded suddenly wary. "Have you been to the surface yet?"

"Not yet. But we're going to go! We hope to visit you, London! To cross the Atlantic!"

"To visit us? Why?"

"So that contact between cities can be restored."

"Perhaps it is best this way," the Londoner said slowly. "We—we are content this way."

"If you don't want contact," Dr. Barnes said, "why did you build the radio set?"

"I did not build it. My cousin Thomas Whitcomb built it. He had—different ideas. He is—dead now . . ."

The set sputtered into incoherence.

"He's saying something!" Jim cried.

Callison scowled, stood up. "We've lost the signal," he said bitterly. There was sudden silence in

4

the room. "I'll try again. But he didn't sound very friendly."

"No," Dr. Barnes said. "He sounded—frightened, almost."

"Maybe someone was monitoring him," suggested Dave Ellis, the short, plump meteorologist. "Maybe he was afraid to say what was on his mind."

"Whitcomb was much more encouraging," Dr. Barnes said.

"Whitcomb's dead," Jim pointed out. "He was killed in an accident."

"I doubt that," Roy Veeder said, in the precise, clipped tones of one who has spent much of his time droning through the dry formalities of the law. "It sounds to me as though Whitcomb were murdered."

Jim stared at the lawyer in shock. "You mean killed deliberately?"

Veeder smiled. "I mean exactly that. I know, it's a strange concept to us. But things like that happened in the old chaotic world up above. And they may still happen in London. I don't think it was an accident. The Londoner was trying to tell us something else. Someone may have deliberately removed Whitcomb. I'm certain that's what he was saying."

Dr. Barnes shrugged. "That may be as may be." He glanced at Callison and said, "Any hope of restoring transmission?"

"I don't think so, Doc. It's dead at the other end. I'm not picking up a thing."

"Try some other channels," Chet Farrington suggested, crossing and recrossing his long legs.

5

"What's the use? No one else is broadcasting."

"Try, at least," Farrington urged.

Callison knelt and began to explore the air waves. After a moment he looked up, his face tense, a muscle flicking in his cheek. "It's a waste of time," he said darkly. "And the air in here stinks! Open that vent a little wider. Seven people and only air enough for two!"

Jim moved toward the vent control. As he started to turn it, his father said simply, "Don't, Jim."

"Ted's right, Dad. The air's bad in here."

"That's okay, Jim. But we don't really want people to know we're meeting, do we? If the computer registers a sudden extra air flow in Ted's room, and somebody bothers to check, we may all have to answer questions."

Callison balled his fist menacingly and shook it at the air vent. "You see?" he demanded of nobody in particular. "We aren't even free to *breathe* down here! Oh, I can't wait to get out! To see the surface, to fill my lungs with real air!"

"It's cold up there, Ted," Dom Hannon said.

"But it's getting warmer!" Callison retorted. "Ask Dave! He'll tell you it's warming up!"

Dave Ellis smiled thinly. "The mean surface temperature is about one degree warmer than it was fifty years ago," he said. "It's warming up there, but not very fast."

"Fast enough," Callison growled. His thick-muscled, powerful body seemed to throb at the injustice of being cooped in a man-made cave far below the surface of the earth. "I want to get out of here," he muttered. "Bad enough that my ancestors were penned down on reservations. But to be boxed up in a little hive underground, to live your whole life without seeing the sky and the clouds—"

"All right," Dave Ellis said with a snort of amused annoyance. "If he's talking about his ancestors, it's time for us to break up for the night. Next thing he'll be painting his face and trying to scalp us, and—"

"Shut your mouth!" Callison erupted. He whirled, amazingly fast for such a thick-set, stocky man, and grabbed the meteorologist by the shoulders. He began to shake him violently. Ellis' head joggled as though it were going to fly loose from its moorings. "I've had enough sarcasm from you!" Callison cried. "If you want to spend the rest of your life huddled like a worm down here, that's all right with me, but—"

"Easy," Ellis gasped. "You're—hurting—me—"

A figure stepped between them and easily separated them—Dr. Barnes, looking fragile but determined as he pushed the chunky Callison away. "Enough of that, Ted," he said quietly.

"It's the air in here," Roy Veeder said crisply. "Stale air makes tempers short."

Dave Ellis rubbed his shoulders ruefully. Still looking angry, Ted Callison began to twiddle the dials of the radio once again, his hands moving in brusque, deliberately jerky gestures.

Jim felt a throb of sympathy for him. The staleness of the air had little to do with the shortness of the tempers in the room, Jim knew. No, it was the tension, the frustration of coming together night

7

after night, of wearily trying to reach someone —anyone—in the outside world, the dull bleak knowledge that you and your descendants to the tenth or twentieth generation were all condemned to spend your lives far underground, hiding from the ice that had conquered the world. The glaciers that covered the surface were like hands at every man's throat.

Callison shut the power off, after a moment. "Nothing," he said. "We've had our talk with London for tonight."

"Too bad about Whitcomb," Ellis said. "He seemed genuinely interested in hearing from us."

"Maybe his cousin is, too," Jim offered. "But he sounded so suspicious—so uneasy."

"Why shouldn't he be?" Callison asked. "Put yourself in his place. You get hold of a radio set that somebody else builds, and you pick up signals from a city nobody's heard from in hundreds of years. They talk about friendship, but do you trust them? Do you trust *anybody*? Suppose this other city is just out to attack you? Lull you into confidence, then steal your nuclear fuel supplies? You never can tell."

"Tom Whitcomb seemed to trust us," Jim said.

"And they must have killed him," Callison said. "I'm sure Roy's right about that. He probably went running to the City Council, or whatever they call it there, and said he had picked up radio signals from New York—so they slit his throat right away, naturally. Men like that are dangerous. They're troublemakers."

Dr. Barnes sighed. "We aren't getting anywhere," he said. "Ted, will you keep trying for an hour or so? If you pick up London again—or anyplace else—let us know."

"Right."

"As for the rest of us," Dr. Barnes said, "we might as well just go back to our rooms."

The group broke up. Jim and his father strode off toward the room they shared, three sections eastward on Level C. Neither of them said much as they walked through the cool, dimly lit corridors. It had been too disappointing an evening to discuss. Hopes that had been high only an hour ago were dashed now.

They had made radio contact with the Londoner, Whitcomb, last week. He had seemed intelligent, alert, a man who enjoyed being alive, a bold and fearless man who welcomed the voice out of the dark. He was dead now. The new voice on the radio had been a more familiar kind of voice, Jim thought—the cramped, edgy voice of fear and mistrust. He knew that kind of voice well.

"It was a pretty rough night, eh, Dad?" Jim said finally, as they reached their room.

"I had hoped for better results," Dr. Barnes admitted. He put his hand to the doorplate, and the sensors recognized his prints. The door yielded. They went in.

The room was small and low of ceiling. There was no space for luxury dwellings in New York. This was not the New York of skyscrapers and stock exchanges, but an underground hive a hundred miles inland from the old Atlantic coastline, a nest of interlocking tunnels going down deep into the crust of the Earth. Eight hundred thousand people lived here. The population had not varied so much as one percentage point in three hundred years. It was not *allowed* to vary. Limiting population was easier than building new tunnels; no laws were more strictly enforced in the underground cities than those controlling population growth.

The room that Jim shared with his father was occupied mostly with microfilmed books, hundreds of reels of them. They belonged to the Central Library—private property was a rarity in underground New York—and Dr. Barnes had nearly filled the room with them. He was writing a history of the twenty-third century, the century in which the Fifth Ice Age came to engulf much of the earth.

Hardly had they closed the door when there came a knock at it. Jim and his father exchanged glances.

"I'll get it, Dad," Jim said.

He opened the door. Ted Callison and Dave Ellis stood there, side by side as though all memory of their recent scuffle had been blotted out.

"What is it?" Jim asked. "Did you pick up London again?"

"No," Callison said. "They've shut down for the night, I guess. Dave and I had an idea, though."

They came in. Dr. Barnes picked up a reel of microfilm, put it down, picked up another, and then another. After a moment of tense silence Dave Ellis said, "Ted and I have decided that radio isn't the right way to reach the Londoners."

"Oh?" Dr. Barnes said.

Callison said, "This way, we're just voices out of nowhere. What we've got to do is go to them. Get up out of the ground and cross the ice and say, 'Here we are, time to thaw out!' The Ice Age is ending. The worst of the freeze is over. We can risk an over-the-ice mission to Europe."

"He's right!" Jim blurted. "Dad, that's the best way."

"It's more than three thousand miles to London," Dr. Barnes said. "No one has made the trip in centuries. No one has left New York in fifty years, even to go to a spot as near as Philadelphia."

"Someone has to start it, Dad!"

"Another point," Dr. Barnes said. "It's taboo to contact other cities. You know that. What we've been doing goes against the whole way of life down here. You don't seriously expect the City Council to welcome the idea of an expedition, do you?"

Ellis said, "We're not asking *them* to go. Just to let *us* go, Dr. Barnes. To outfit us with such equipment as they can give us for the expedition. With a little help, we can make it to London. We can—"

There was another knock at the door. Jim frowned; his father gestured with a thumb, and Jim went to open it. Somehow, irrationally, he was expecting trouble, and trouble was there—in the form of four husky young men wearing the brassards of the police.

Jim knew one of them, at least slightly. He was Carl Bolin, a broad-shouldered, blond-haired young man, whose father, Peter Bolin, had been a hydroponics technician and instructor. Jim had studied with the elder Bolin the previous year, and had met Carl several times. Only a few months before, Jim had been saddened by Peter Bolin's death, and had sent condolences to Carl. And now here Carl was with three of his police comrades, and not here to visit, either. He looked both sheepish and grim at the same time, as though he were embarrassed by his mission and yet determined to carry it out.

One of the other policemen stepped forward. "Dr. Barnes? I'm sorry to say, you're under arrest. Also your son James. I'm instructed to take you to City Council headquarters." His hand went to the butt of his stun gun in a meaningful gesture. "I hope you'll surrender peacefully, sir."

A second policeman eyed Callison and Ellis. "Your names?" he demanded.

"Ted Callison."

"Dave Ellis."

"Very convenient, finding you two here. We've got warrants for both of you, also. Come along."

Jim saw Ted Callison's muscles tensing under his thin green shirt, and realized that the hothead was likely to cause trouble. Quietly, Jim reached out and caught Callison's thick wrist, encircling it with his fingers and squeezing until he heard Ted grunt.

"Don't do anything," Jim murmured.

Callison subsided, grumbling under his breath.

Dr. Barnes said, "We're entitled to know the nature of the charges against us, aren't we?"

The first policeman nodded somberly. "The charge is treason, Dr. Barnes."

# 2

## *Enemies of the City*

DOWN, DOWN, DOWN!

Down through the coiling intestines of the underground city, down through level after level, down past the last residential level to the industrial levels, and then still down, down to Level M in the depths of the city, the administrative level where no one went except on official business.

Here, the great computer that co-ordinated the life of the city ticked and throbbed. Here, the master controls of the city were housed: the water-recycling factory and the air plant and the food-processing laboratories and the hydroponics sheds. Here, too, was City Hall, where the Mayor and his nine Councilors ran the city.

Jim had been here once, when he was twelve, on a school trip. Every civics class came here once to be shown the heart and core of New York. He had seen, and he had been awed. Now he was here again—a prisoner.

The gleaming shell of the elevator came to a halt.

"Out," the police ordered.

Out, and down a shining ramp, and into a waiting roller car that ran along a track down a wide corridor, through looping curves of hallway. Dimly visible to left and to right were bulky power plants and mysterious installations, flat against the low ceiling. A faint humming sound, ominous and persistent, assailed Jim's ears. The deep booming *thum*-thum *thum*-thum *thum*-thum of the generators set a rhythm for his own thumping heart. Every narrow corridor intersecting the main one bore a glowing sign:

AUTHORIZED PERSONNEL ONLY

Some of the signs carried an extra symbol, the atom-symbol, warning that this was the approach to the nuclear reactor that powered the entire city. Anyone caught going beyond a sign that bore the atom-symbol was a dead man if a guard saw him. No citizen could approach the reactor for any reason whatever, without express permission of the City Council. To cross into the forbidden zone was to invite a fatal full-intensity blast from a stun gun, no questions asked.

There was silence in the roller car. Dr. Barnes sat in the front seat, bolt upright between two of the policemen. Jim, Ted Callison, and Dave Ellis were crowded together with a third policeman in the rear seat, while the remaining officer was hunched behind them, his stun gun drawn, its blunt snout tickling their backbones warningly. Jim saw Callison's powerful fists clenching and unclenching in cold, silent fury.

City Hall loomed up before them, squat and somehow sinister. The roller car halted. More police were waiting there, at least a dozen of them, although by now it was quite late at night.

"Out," came the crisp order.

The four prisoners left the roller car, hands held high. The new escort moved in, surrounding them, and the original police drove off. The prisoners were marched into City Hall, and down the brightly lit hallway that Jim had seen five years before.

He had met Mayor Hawkes then, and had been terrified of the seam-faced, wizened old man who had governed New York for what seemed like all eternity. Then, the Mayor had beamed, had smiled at the class of edgy twelve-year-olds, and had welcomed them all to the city's administrative level.

Mayor Hawkes would not beam tonight, Jim thought.

"In here," a frog-voiced policeman said crisply.

*Here* turned out to be a square, forbidding little room whose unnaturally bright illumination stung the eyes. There was a raised dais along the far wall, and a low table with a bench behind it. No other furniture broke the starkness of the room. There were three other prisoners there already—Roy Veeder, Dom Hannon, Chet Farrington. The whole

15

group, then—all seven who had gathered around the little radio to hear the squeaky voice from London only a short while before.

Rounded up! Charged with treason!

A door slid back out of sight, recessing into the rear wall, and a new group of men entered. Old men. Mayor Hawkes led the way, wearing his official robes of office for the occasion, the blue cloak with the orange trim, the peaked hat, the seal of power dangling from a massive chain around his neck.

He looked horribly, grotesquely old. He had been Mayor of New York since 2611, thirty-nine years ago, and he had been a middle-aged man when first elected. Every ten years since he had been re-elected, and everyone assumed that he would be elected without opposition to a fifth term next year, though he was now nearly ninety. He stood rigidly erect, the light glaring down on his domed, wrinkled forehead, his hook of a nose, his withered cheeks and sharp chin. Humorless pale blue eyes glinted deep in the Mayor's eye sockets.

Behind him marched the City Council, nine of them, the youngest well past sixty. Like the mayor, the City Council was supposedly chosen in open election every ten years. But it had been a century or more since anyone had last contested an election. The way the system worked now, a new Councilor was elected only when one of the old ones died—and the stubborn old men never seemed to die. Two of the nine were past the hundred-year mark now, and evidently planned to live forever.

The ten rulers of New York arrayed themselves along the dais and sat down. Ten pairs of flinty aged eyes peered in hostility at the prisoners, who stood before them.

Dr. Barnes said, staring straight at the Mayor, "Your Honor, I demand to know the meaning of this arrest."

"The charge is treason," Mayor Hawkes said in a voice that sounded like a swinging rusty gate. "The seven of you have engaged in activities detrimental to the welfare of New York City, and you stand accused. How do you plead?"

Jim gasped. His father said, "Is this a trial?"

"It is."

"Without lawyers? Without witnesses? Without a judge or a jury?"

"I understand there is one among you who is a lawyer," the Mayor replied, with a glance at Roy Veeder. "He can speak for you. I am the judge. The Council is the jury. There is no need for anyone else."

"You know we have the right of independent counsel, Your Honor," Roy Veeder said. "An accused man is entitled—"

"Never mind, Roy," Dr. Barnes said. "They have us, and we're helpless."

"No." Veeder shook his head. "I must protest, Your Honor," he said to the Mayor. "This violates the basic charter of the city. Accused men have right of counsel. You are not empowered to conduct a trial, Your Honor! Your powers are executive, not judicial!"

"Roy's wasting his breath," Ted Callison murmured to Jim. "Those men can do anything they please. This is a trial that was over before it ever began."

Jim nodded. A sense of hopeless rage stole over

him. Those ten willful men up there had ruled the city so long they were convinced of their own infallibility. What did charters, laws, codes mean to them? They were the representatives of the people! They were the rulers!

The Mayor's taunt, fleshless face grew harsher, more ugly. He glowered at Roy Veeder and said, "Such trial as you will have, you will have here, Counselor Veeder. If you object to the proceedings, you will be removed from the room and tried *in absentia*. Traitors must be dealt with promptly. It is late at night."

"Of course," Ted Callison blurted out. "Old men need to get their sleep! Get rid of us fast so you can get to bed!"

Callison grunted as the snout of a stun gun was rammed into his kidneys. He subsided. There was a chill silence in the room. The Mayor beckoned, and the sliding panel opened again. A policeman walked in—carrying the radio!

He carried it as though it were a live serpent. He put it down on the table before the Mayor, and backed out of the room.

The Mayor eyed the square box sourly, then glared at the prisoners. "With this," he said, "you contacted another city. You spoke with men from London. True or false?"

"True," Roy said.

"You conspired with them against the welfare of New York City. You plotted the overthrow of the legally constituted government of this city."

"That's false, Your Honor," Roy said.

"There is evidence on record against you."

"Produce it, then! It's an established principle of

law that an accused man has the right to be confronted with evidence on which he's been indicted."

"There is no need of that," the Mayor said, almost to himself. "The evidence exists. We have examined it and discussed it. Traitors! Enemies of the city!"

"No," Dr. Barnes said. "We are not traitors! I won't deny we've been in contact with London. Dave Ellis, here, has been studying surface conditions with the telemetering equipment. He believes that the Freeze is almost over, that climatic conditions have reversed themselves at last. It's time to come up out of the ground. Time for men to breathe the air again, to walk under the open sky. And so we've tried to reach other cities, to find out what's been happening in the world. All this I freely admit. But treason? No! Enemies of the city? No!"

"You are trying to disturb the established order of things," the Mayor said cuttingly. "This is treason, and must be punished. You stand condemned by your own words. I call for the verdict, Councilors."

"Guilty!" came the hoarse croaking sounds of the old men. "Guilty! Guilty! Guilty!"

The Mayor's thin lips drew back in a cold smile. "The verdict is guilty," he said. "It is late. Take them away, guards. We will announce the sentence in the morning."

The trial was over.

The mockery of justice had lasted less than ten minutes.

Guilty!

19

Enemies of the city!

Jim Barnes paced tensely around the cell that he shared with Roy Veeder, Dave Ellis and Chet Farrington. His father, Ted Callison, and Dom Hannon were next door.

The verdict had not surprised him. He had known what the prevailing patterns of thought in the city were, had known that the clandestine radio contact with London might be considered treasonable. What angered him was not the verdict so much as the cynical dispatch with which the "trial" had been conducted. It had been no trial, simply an out-of-hand condemnation by a small group of autocratic, self-centered old dodderers.

In a few hours sentence would be imposed. Jim wondered what it would be. In the old days, he knew, men had frequently been put to death by their governments for crimes. Thank Heaven that bit of barbarity had gone out with the Dark Ages, he thought. Punishment for crime today was more civilized, though hardly a cheerful matter.

There were few serious crimes in New York. Since no one had much personal property, theft was all but unknown. Murder was unheard-of. Disputes still arose, people frequently lost their tempers—but, in the stable, tightly regulated underground city, there wasn't much scope for wrongdoing. Such serious crimes as were committed were punished, first of all, by loss of parenthood privileges. Every resident of the city was considered to have the right to give life to one child, his own replacement—no more. A criminal might have that right suspended, or even taken away permanently. Then, too, punishments included loss of free-time privileges, demotion to less desirable living quarters, job degradation. Jim wondered if he and his father would be sentenced to a year or two of manning the garbage conduits.

No, he thought. Somehow he expected a graver sentence.

The night ticked away. Jim tried to sleep, but it was no use. He boiled with rage. The fear of the Mayor he had felt when he was twelve had given way to hatred now.

The stupid, stubborn, mindless, tyrannical old man!

Jim, his father, Ted Callison, and the others had discussed the psychology of the city many times during the long hours of working on the radio. They had all attacked the prevailing attitudes bluntly, as they would not dare to do among strangers.

"It's a withdrawal pattern," Dr. Barnes had said. "A kind of isolationism. Here we are, snug in our little burrow under the ice, and anybody who wants to climb out of the hole in the ground is obviously a subversive and a traitor."

"But the underground cities were supposed to be only temporary refuges," Ted Callison had pointed out. "Places for civilization to endure until the ice sheets retreated."

"Ah, yes!" Dr. Barnes had grinned. "But it's too comfortable down here. The machinery purrs along smoothly, population growth is regulated, every person has his niche in society. There are no troublesome challenges."

"Like a city full of ostriches," Chet Farrington said. And then, seeing the blank faces, he added in

21

explanation, "A large flightless bird. It hides its head in the sand when it's faced with trouble it doesn't want to see."

It was true, Jim thought. The builders of the underground cities have done their work well, and the cities would endure for thousands of years. There was no need to venture up to the frozen surface. Why look for trouble? Why—to use an expression long since obsolete—why rock the boat?

Even in a city where boats were unknown, the expression had meaning. Ted Callison and Dr. Barnes and Jim and the others were boat-rockers. They were not content to live out their lives placidly underground. They yearned to return to the surface world, now that the ice had reached its peak spread and was beginning to retreat. They longed to see that strange world above, to explore its vastness. It was time to reach out for contact with survivors in other cities—if any.

The world had begun to grow cold about the year 2200. It had started gradually, with an ever-so-slight drop in the annual mean temperature all over the world. For several centuries prior to that, the world had been growing warmer, and the idea of a Fifth Ice Age had seemed fantastic—until it began to happen.

Four times in the geologically recent past, the last million years, glaciers had descended on the world. Many ingenious theories had been offered to explain those glacial periods. Changes in the solar radiation, increases or decreases in the carbon dioxide content of the atmosphere, variations in the temperature of the Arctic Ocean—all these theories had been put forth, and each had its advocates.

In 2200, the world again began to grow cold.

The change was stealthy. Winters were longer by a few days each year. In parts of the world where the warmth of spring once had come by the middle of March, it did not come until early April. The summers were cooler. Where snow had previously fallen no earlier than late November, it began to fall in October, then in late September. The snow was more abundant, too.

In the arctic regions, summer disappeared altogether after a while. There was no midyear warmth to melt the winter snows. The ice accumulated, hundreds of feet thick across the top of the world, and as the weight increased, the ice began to flow. Glaciers—rivers of ice—crept southward across Canada, and down out of Scandinavia into Europe.

"The winters are getting colder," people said, but it was twenty years before anyone realized that a major trend was under way. Each year the mean temperature was a fraction of a degree lower than it had been the year before. Some villages of Alaska, Canada, and Sweden had to be evacuated as the glaciers crept down toward them.

By 2230, everyone knew what was happening, and why. The sun and all its planets, it was found, as they moved together through the universe had been engulfed by a vast cloud of cosmic debris, and an all but infinite number of dust motes were screening and blocking the sun's radiation from Earth. To the eye, everything still looked the same; the sky was just as blue, the clouds as fleecy. The cosmic dust could not be seen, but its effect could be felt. Invisible, it shrouded the sun, cut off the golden warmth. And so immense was the cloud that it would take centuries for the Solar System to pass entirely through it!

An Ice Age would result.

The temperature of Earth would continue to drop. Not drastically, true. Just enough to insure that more snow fell every winter than could be melted in the warm months. As the accumulations built up, glaciers would crawl out of the north, other glaciers would lick the tip of South America and rise from Patagonia. Half the world would be buried beneath the ice.

There were plans aplenty for halting the glaciers, of course. Atomic-powered heating plants were suggested. Melt the ice, funnel it into the sea!

The plans were tested, run off by simulator computers. Ten years of study culminated in the melancholy realization that man was powerless against the advancing ice. Proud twenty-third-century man, lord of creation, was powerless!

It would take every bit of fissionable material in the world to defeat the ice. Such gigantic quantities of water would be liberated that the seas of the world would rise six to ten feet, drowning the world's greatest cities. The radiation products from the atomic heaters would poison man's environment.

Nothing could hold back the ice. Nothing!

People began to flee. The ice shield ground inexorably down, and mass migrations began, millions of people heading southward before the white front of the invader. Naturally, everyone wanted to settle in those countries that would not feel the brunt of the glaciation, the countries along the Equator. Brazil, the Congo, Nigeria, Algeria, India, Indonesia—these became the new powers of the world. Russia, China, the United States all were crippled by the cold. The tropical lands, though, benefited. Their climate grew cool and moist, pleasant, ideal for agriculture and industrialization. Rain fell in the Sahara; the desert bloomed. Wheat fields sprouted in the Amazon basin.

The tropical countries closed their doors to immigrants. "We do not need you," they told the refugees from the North. "We do not want you."

The highly industrialized, powerful new nations along the waistline of the world were strong enough to make their isolationist policies stick. Despair and dismay swept the people of the once-temperate zones. Thousands perished in riots —food riots, work riots, and motiveless riots of sheer fright and anguish. The birth rates dropped, for who would bring children into a world of gathering cold, a world without food? In a single thirty-year span, the population of the United States fell from 280,000,000 to 240,000,000—and it kept on falling.

Since there was no way to roll back the ice, one could only hide from it. The nations of the glacier-menaced countries began to go underground. Self-contained, atomic-powered cities were built, capable of surviving under the ice for an indefinite length of time. Twenty such cities were built in the United States, and they were given time-hallowed names like Chicago and Boston, Philadelphia and New York, Detroit and Washington, even though they were usually far from the sites of those surface cities. In Europe, too, many cities went underground.

Not everyone chose to go down into the ground. Many decided to try their luck as wanderers, roaming the face of the storm-blasted world in the hopes that the nations of the warm belt would relent and take them in.

The new cities were built slowly, and with care. There was no real hurry, since the ice was advancing only a few miles a year. The underground city of New York was ready for occupancy in the year 2297, about a century after the Earth had entered the cloud of cosmic dust. By that time, only a million and a half people were left in New York; millions had already fled the increasingly bitter winters, only to cluster helplessly at the closed southern borders. The new underground city was built to hold eight hundred thousand. Less than five hundred thousand New Yorkers agreed to take refuge there. The city was sealed, and the ice covered it.

And now it was 2650 A.D., and the underground cities were more than three hundred years old. They slumbered under a mile-high blanket of ice. They had long since lost contact with one another, and by now all such contact was taboo. The New Yorkers, whose number had grown to 800,000 and then had been fixed there by law, were warm and happy in their underground hive. Who cared for the outside world? Why go back to the vale of tears?

Taboo!

Taboo to repair one of the old radio sets. Taboo to seek contact with another city. Taboo to dream of a day when men would again walk above-ground, under the warm yellow sun.

The Earth *was* growing warmer again, unless the instruments Dave Ellis used had lied. It was time to be stirring, time to go forth. But . . .

Taboo!

Jim Barnes looked up at the roof of his cell, only a foot or so above his head. He stood six feet two, no height for a man who lived underground. The walls and low ceilings oppressed him. He yearned to be out.

The cell door whirred open. Morning had come.

"This way," the policeman said.

"What about breakfast?" Chet Farrington asked.

"We've got no food for the likes of you here! Just come with us!"

The prisoners assembled in the corridor. Jim nodded good morning to his father, who rather grimly smiled a greeting. The shadows under Dr. Barnes's eyes showed that he, too, had slept little.

They were marched down the hall, into the room where the "trial" had been held the night before. The Mayor and his Council had already gathered. The prisoners took their places, lined up before the parchment-skinned oldsters.

Mayor Hawkes rose to his feet, swaying a little. His voice, though, was steady.

He said, "You are dangerous men. You threaten the security of the entire city. What are we to do with you? To put you to death would be an atrocity. To keep you here, though, would be extremely foolish. One does not store live bombs in one's own home." A mirthless smile played over the thin, pale lips. "What to do with you?" the Mayor

27

repeated. "What to do with you? We have deliberated for hours. And we have reached our decision."

He paused and the cold blue eyes raked the row of silent prisoners.

He said, "Dr. Barnes, you have told me of your great wish to contact other cities, to explore the surface world. Very well. You shall have your wish. I sentence all of you to expulsion from New York City. You are to leave the city within twelve hours. If you return, you will be treated as enemy invaders, which is to say you will be put to death."

Ted Callison laughed. "Why not just throw us into the atomic reactor and get it over with quickly? It's a faster death than sending us outside, isn't it?"

"I thought you and your group were eager to see the outside world," the Mayor said coolly.

"In a properly equipped expedition, yes. Not cast forth helpless!" Callison retorted.

Mayor Hawkes looked positively benevolent. "Did I say we would send you out of here naked? That would be a death sentence, and we do not have the death sentence here. You will be properly equipped, all of you. If you perish on the surface, it will not be our fault. We are not cruel men. We have the safety of the city foremost in our minds —and so you must leave. But we are not cruel men." The Mayor laughed, almost a senile giggle. Then he sat down. He waved his hand petulantly. "Take them away," he snapped. "They have twelve hours to get out!"

## 3

# To the Surface!

"IT'S ON THE BOOKS," DR. BARNES SAID. "EXPULSION from the city is the punishment for a crime against the city."

"But that law hasn't been enforced in decades," Dave Ellis said. "When was the last expulsion, anyway?"

"Twenty-five ninety-three," Roy Veeder said. "It's a historic case. I studied it in law school. A man named Stanton was expelled for advocating that everybody ought to have as many children as he wanted. That was the last one. What's more, it's the last time *anybody* left New York, voluntarily or otherwise—in fifty-seven years!"

"We'll die out there," Dave Ellis muttered.

"What makes you so sure?" Jim snapped at him. "Just last evening, you were all set to go on an expedition to the surface!"

Ellis shook his head. The pudgy meteorologist was downcast and fearful now. He knotted his plump fingers together tensely. "I was talking about a proper expedition," he said. "One that had months of planning. Surveys of the surface to test conditions up there. Special equipment. And now, here they are, just throwing us out. Poof! Twelve hours to plan the whole thing!"

Dr. Barnes said, "We'll manage, somehow. There's no sense giving up in advance. Pull yourself together, Dave!"

Ted Callison nodded. "We'll make it!" he said fiercely. "We'll make it all the way to London. Three thousand miles—what's that? If we can hike twenty miles a day we can get there in less than six months!"

"Why go all the way to London?" Dom Hannon asked, nervously fingering his thinning hair. "There are cities closer at hand. Boston. Philadelphia."

"We don't know anything about them," Jim said. "For all we can tell, everyone's been dead in those cities for two hundred years. We couldn't raise them on the radio. At least we know London's alive. We've talked to people there. Ted's right: we'll have to try to make it to London."

"Three thousand miles," Dave Ellis murmured feebly. "It isn't possible!"

"We're going to make it possible," Ted Callison said.

* * *

One thing, at least, could be said for the Mayor and the City Councilors: they were not deliberately trying to send the condemned men to their deaths. They were willing to supply the outcasts with whatever New York City had available in the way of survival equipment. Which was not very much. No one had been out of the city since before the turn of the century, and the warm clothing, the tents, the signal flares, and all the rest of the surface-going material had been stored as museum pieces.

In the hours that remained to them, Jim and his father and the rest of their group rummaged desperately through the storehouse on Level M, taking what they thought they would need. The Councilors were kind enough, at least, to let them take their radio. New York had no need of such things.

It was only now, in the final hours before leaving New York City, that Jim began to realize what a slim chance of survival they all had. Not one of them had ever been exposed to weather below sixty-eight degrees, for the temperature in the underground city was never allowed to fall below that point. None of them had ever covered a distance of more than a mile on foot, for there was nowhere to walk any great length in the city of tunnels. None of them had hunted for food. None of them had any experience at all in the techniques of survival under adverse conditions.

*We'll be babes in the woods*, Jim thought.

No help for it now. They would simply have to learn survival as they went along—or else.

The day was drawing to its close by the time they had assembled their equipment. The two prizes were a pair of jet-sleds that could each seat five

31

men comfortably, plus baggage. At least they would not have to cross the trackless wastes on foot! A search through the city archives produced an instruction manual for the sleds; they had a copy made.

Knives, hatchets, tinned provisions and a six-month supply of food pellets, glare-goggles, compasses, sextants, power torches—no, they were not exactly going forth naked into the wilderness. But their total lack of experience with surface conditions would make every moment incalculably hazardous.

There were no good-bys. The trial had happened too fast. Not until the condemned men were outside would the people of the city be told of what had taken place. That is, if they were told at all. One could never be sure that the Mayor would see fit to release the news. Seven citizens had "disappeared," and no one would be the wiser for it. In a world where the largest families had two children —under rare circumstances, three—there were few family alliances, few relatives to ponder the disappearances. Dr. Barnes's wife had died when Jim was a baby; none of the other outcasts had ever been married.

It was early in the evening when the moment of departure came. The expedition had assembled its belongings in Level A, near the hatch that led upward to the surface world. They were only a hundred feet below the old surface. But a mile or more of ice lay between them and the open sky.

A contingent of police escorted them from the city. Carl Bolin was one of them.

Surprisingly enough, a couple of the young policemen looked enviously at the departing group. And as Jim lugged a folded tent toward the hatch, Carl came up alongside and said, "Let me give you a hand with that, Jim."

"I can manage."

"But I can help you." Carl seized the back half of the bulky, cumbersome tent and together they lugged it toward the hatch. The policeman said quietly to Jim, "You don't know how lucky you are. I wish I was going with you!"

"Who's stopping you?"

"I can't go. I—I've got a job here. I—" Carl hesitated, and looked strangely at his police brassard. "It would be desertion," he muttered. "I'm a policeman! An officer of the law. And the law—"

"—is sending us outside," Jim said. "We can use another strong back."

"It wouldn't be right to leave," Carl insisted. "They wouldn't let me go, anyway. I've had police training. I owe it to the city to stay here and serve."

"Suit yourself," Jim answered curtly.

It took half an hour to move everything through the hatch into the musty, dusty tunnel outside. The hardest part was getting the two jet-sleds through; they were almost as wide as the hatch itself, and had to be maneuvered delicately. During the building of the city, many openings hundreds of feet wide had been left to permit the entry of construction materials and machinery, but they had all been sealed, all but this small opening, through which only a few could pass at a time. Jim wondered what would happen if it ever became necessary to evacuate New York suddenly. But that was no longer his problem, he told himself. He and New York City were at the parting of the ways.

33

"Everything set?" asked the policeman in charge.

Dr. Barnes nodded. "We've got all our gear through."

"Close the hatch, then!"

The seven outcasts stood amid their heaps of belongings in the vestibule beyond the hatch. Three burly policemen began to swing the heavy door closed. It moved smoothly enough on its burnished gimbals. Jim felt a pounding in his heart as it swung into place. Another two yards and the hatch would be closed, and they would be banished from New York City forever. . . .

"Wait!" someone yelled.

An instant later, a figure slipped through the hatch and into the vestibule to join the exiles: Carl, the young policeman. He made it with only seconds to spare, and just as the hatch slammed shut, he ripped the police brassard from his arm and flipped it through the narrow opening, back into the city from which he had just exiled himself.

*Clang!*

The hatch was closed now. From the far side came the sounds of metal rasping against metal as the police dogged the hatch in place. There was no return possible. The barrier could be opened only from the inside.

"I want to go with you," Carl said to Dr. Barnes.

Jim's father smiled faintly. "It looks as though we have no choice but to accept you. Who are you?"

"Carl Bolin. My father was Peter Bolin the hydroponics technician."

"I know him, Dad," Jim said. "He's all right."

"He'd better be," Dr. Barnes said, and there was

a strange coldness to his tone that startled Jim. "Everybody in this team is going to have to pull his own weight. We can't make allowances for slackers."

Ted Callison peered upward into the dimness above them. "We'd better start loading the elevator," he said. "Time to get moving."

Jim shared his impatience. The outside world, that forbidding land of snow and ice, was only a legend to him. Neither he nor his father, nor even his grandfather's grandfather, had ever set eyes on that world. Of the eight of them, only Dave Ellis had ever had a glimpse of the surface, and that had been at second hand, through one of the periscopes the meteorologists used. During the centuries underground, the city's meteorologists had come to have an almost religious role. It was they, and they alone, who were permitted to monitor surface conditions, using telemetering devices and periscopic television eyes. The city's Charter expressly commanded that the surveillance continue ceaselessly. The idea was, of course, that the city should be prepared for the day when the surface became habitable again.

But with the passing of the decades the meteorologists' role had become purely ritualistic. Nobody seriously expected man ever to return to the surface again—except for a few dreamers like Dr. Barnes and Jim. Each month, the meteorologists made their observations, and formally submitted their report to the Mayor—and the report was just as formally filed away, unread, merely part of the ritual.

Maybe, Jim thought, the reason Dave was so apprehensive about the surface was the fact that he, alone among them, had some idea of what it was really like.

An elevator ran up the side of the tunnel that led to the surface. Through the years, the tunnel had been extended up into the gathering ice pack, and it had been a sacred duty of the city dwellers to keep the passage clear. Jim suspected, though, that no tunnel maintenance had been performed in years. Would they be able to get out to the surface after all? Suppose miles of ice pinned them down? Where would they go? New York would not take them back.

"Everything's aboard the elevator," Roy Veeder called out.

"Let's hope it still works," Dr. Barnes said. "Ted, can you reach the switch?"

"Got it."

There was a groaning, a whining, as servo motors spun into life after decades of inactivity. The elevator seemed to strain against its moorings. Had its core rotted away, or was the load simply too great for it?

"Maybe we'll have to make two trips," Dom Hannon suggested. "The elevator's carrying a couple of tons, and—"

And it began to lift.

Slowly, painfully, it rose away from the tunnel floor and began to toil toward the surface.

The eight men on the elevator's open platform huddled together. It was cold, in the tunnel shaft, and it grew colder as they rose. Was it simply the chill of the upper world, Jim wondered, or was it an inner chill that made the goose pimples rise along his skin?

"We're up a hundred twenty feet," Ted Callison reported. "We must be into the glacier now."

"Shine a light upward," Dr. Barnes said. "Let's see how far up the shaft is clear."

It was impossible to tell. Light gleamed along the shiny metal walls of the tunnel, and it was apparent that the way was open for at least several hundred feet more above them. But beyond that . . . ?

The elevator continued to rise.

Jim glanced at Carl Bolin. The brawny young ex-policeman was gripping the edge of one of the sleds, holding on for dear life. His eyes were closed, and his lips were moving as if in prayer. Jim felt like praying himself. Suppose the elevator failed, and dashed them hundreds of feet back down to the tunnel floor? Or suppose a plug of ice dozens of yards thick blocked them from reaching the surface?

Jim drew his parka close about him. He had never worn warm clothing before, and the bulk of the heavy garment oppressed him. So, too, the idea of the bulk of the ice above him oppressed him. Millions of tons of frozen water, pressing down. He had never really thought of it that way before. The ice had been simply something that was there, something taken for granted. But now he felt as though the whole great weight of the glacier lay upon his back.

Upward.

"It's dark above us!" Ted Callison called out. "The tunnel's closed, and we've only gone four hundred feet!"

A stab of the flashlight revealed, though, that the

37

darkness above them was caused by a metal hatch set athwart the tunnel, and not by a plug of ice. Obviously the builders of the tunnel to the surface had partitioned it with horizontal bulkheads so that possible melting ice from above would not flood the lower part of the tunnel. But would the hatch open?

The elevator ground to a halt. It was possible to peer over the edge and see the vestibule, tiny and dark, hundreds of feet below. After a few moments of inspection, Jim came upon a set of switches mounted in the tunnel wall. A hasty conference followed; then Ted Callison threw one of the switches.

The hatch began to swing open.

Creaking and protesting, the thick door re-tracted until it had withdrawn itself half the width of the tunnel. There was room for the elevator to continue upward. Callison started the elevator again. When they passed through the bulkhead, they found more switches, and one of them closed the hatch. They moved on toward the surface.

Four hundred feet farther up, they came to another hatch, and passed it the same way. Then a third, and a fourth, and a fifth. More than half a mile separated them now from the entrance to New York City, and—hopefully—only half a mile separated them from the surface.

This was the newest part of the tunnel, built only some two hundred years before. There were subtle changes in the workmanship. It became more slipshod, as though this part of the tunnel had been put in purely out of ritualistic reflex, rather than out of any real intention ever to use it for a mass exodus from the city.

Upward. Upward. Past a sixth hatch, and a seventh.

Then, as they drew near the eighth bulkhead, it became apparent that the next barrier was not a man-made one. A ceiling of ice blocked the shaft!

They halted the elevator within fifteen feet of the ceiling. By climbing up on the sled and stretching, Jim could just barely touch the ice. He put his finger tips to it, and drew them away quickly, as though burned.

"Cold!"

"Yes," Dr. Barnes said, "and it'll be a lot colder for us if we're stuck in this tunnel forever. Break out the power torches!"

Roy Veeder and Chet Farrington unpacked one of the knapsacks and produced four power torches, yard-long metal rods whose tiny fusion plasmas generated fierce heat. Dr. Barnes studied the ice plug thoughtfully.

"We don't want to bring it down on our heads," he said. "Let's melt away the far side of it first and see what happens."

Jim took one of the torches, his father another. Dr. Barnes hefted his torch and pressed the firing stud. A greenish glow of light bathed the surface of the ice plug, which melted away as though touched by a dragon's fiery breath. In the chill of the tunnel, the ice vapor condensed a moment later, and the men on the elevator heard a sound brand-new to them: that of rain, falling from a highly localized cloud and pelting down hundreds of feet to the closed metal hatch below them.

"Listen to it!" Carl whispered. "Little drops of water falling! Like a hundred drums!"

The power torch had bitten a gouge twenty feet

39

high and six or seven feet across into the ice plug. It held firm.

Dave Ellis said, "Someone left the city at the turn of the century. That fellow Stanton that Roy mentioned. We haven't found any bones along the way, so he must have come at least this far. Therefore the ice above us is less than a sixty-year accumulation."

"How thick would that be, Dave?" Dr. Barnes asked.

Ellis shook his head. "There are five or six feet of snow a year in these parts now. But the question isn't so much the amount that falls as the amount that doesn't melt. The year-to-year accumulation may be as much as a couple of feet—or it could be less."

"So we may have fifty to a hundred feet of ice above us," Dr. Barnes said. "All right. Everybody pull up hoods. We're going to get wet."

He gripped the power torch again, and this time aimed it straight overhead. The lambent glow of the torch turned the tunnel bright; another slice of ice disappeared; cold droplets of rain showered down on the roofless elevator. Jim shivered, but grinned all the same, and turned his face upward to the rain. He saw Ted Callison, hoodless, all but capering in the icy shower.

The beam licked out again. And again. Thirty feet of air space gaped above them where a few moments before there had been a roof of ice. But the ice seemed as thick, as dark as ever. What if it were half a mile thick? A mile?

"Lift the elevator twenty feet, Ted," Dr. Barnes ordered. "I'm getting out of range."

The elevator rose slowly. The power torch flared again. Rain showered down.

Up. Up.

Then the torch spurted cold fire, there was a sudden sizzle, and chunks of ice began to hail down on them, chunks six inches, a foot across.

"The plug's breaking!" Jim yelled, shielding himself from the massive chunks.

A moment later, the fall ceased. "Everyone okay?" Dr. Barnes asked. "I went right through the roof. Look up!"

Jim looked. And gasped.

The plug was broken. Fragments of ice still clung to the sides of the tunnel, but there was a gaping hole twenty feet across, through which could be seen a flat swatch of blackness, and little dots of light so sharp and hard they hurt the eyes, and the edge of a great gleaming thing, painfully bright.

The night sky!

The stars!

The moon!

"Hoist the elevator, Ted," Dr. Barnes yelled. "Hoist it! We're at the surface! We've made it!"

_____ **4**

# The White Desert

IT WAS A SILENT WORLD OF BLINDING WHITENESS.

It was a cold world.

Jim hoisted himself over the rim of the tunnel mouth, stepped into the new world, and fought back a surge of panic as he saw the magnitude of it all. Even at night, even by moonlight, it was possible to see how the flat ice sheet spread out to the horizon. It was a numbing, breath-taking sight for anyone who had spent his whole life in tunnels hardly higher than his head.

And the whiteness of it! The fierce dazzle of the moonlight as it bounced and glittered from the fields of snow!

The world blazed. It sparkled. It shimmered with light.

One by one, the men were coming up out of the tunnel. Carl emerged, and cringed in disbelief at the immensity of the ice field. He put his hands to his eyes, shielding them against the glare of the moon and the stars, and hastily donned his goggles.

"It's cold," he whispered. "So cold!"

Dave Ellis appeared, looking tense and apprehensive. Roy Veeder, Chet Farrington, Dom Hannon. Dr. Barnes. Then Ted Callison, even his high spirits dampened by the sudden emergence into the world. The eight stood together, uncertain, confused.

Jim knelt. He touched the ground—gingerly, for he remembered how the ice had burned. What he touched was stingingly cold, but he was prepared for the shock this time.

"See," he said. "There's white powder everywhere."

"Snow," Dave Ellis said. "Six, seven inches of snow lying on the ice. It's springtime. Most of the winter snow has melted and refrozen, and become part of the glacier." He kicked at the fluffy snow, sending a cloud of it into the air. "There's just this little layer of snow on top."

Ted Callison bent, gathered snow in both hands, sent it soaring into the air. The flakes floated down, shining like diamonds in the bright moonlight. He scooped again, and showers of snow cascaded down.

"Careful," Dr. Barnes said. "Put your gloves on. Your skin isn't designed for these temperatures."

43

"How cold do you think it is, anyway, Dad?" Jim asked.

"Dave can tell you that."

The meteorologist had already started to examine his thermometer. He was carrying what amounted to a portable weather station, snug in his parka.

"Not too bad," he retorted after a moment. "It's twenty-two above zero. It may even be above freezing by morning. It's a fine spring night."

Jim shivered. A scything gust of wind swept down on them, and seemed to cut through his bulky clothes as though they were gauze. A lucky thing they were making this trip in spring, he thought. In winter, Dave said, the temperature ranged between forty below zero and ten above. Forty below! The mere thought of it made his teeth chatter.

But he was warm in a little while, as they busied themselves breaking out the jet-sleds and bundling their belongings aboard. There was nowhere they could go until morning; the energy accumulators of the sleds were solar-powered, and had long since run down, so that a couple of hours of charging by daylight would be necessary before they could get going. And morning was still three or four hours away.

Roy Veeder and Ted Callison pitched a tent, and some of them settled down to wait for sunrise. Jim was still too restless to sleep. He had had nothing but quick naps for the past two days, and fatigue made his red-rimmed eyes raw and foggy, but the wonder of the white new world burned the sleep from him, and left him throbbing with excitement, tense as a coiled spring.

He walked away from the group, moving cautiously, his booted feet sinking half a foot or more into the loose, drifting snow before they struck the reassuring solidity of the glacier beneath. The cold air assailed his lungs, stung his nostrils. But it was a joy to breathe it. There was a freshness about it that dizzied him; it was as tangy and sweet as new wine. He halted in the snow, a hundred feet from his party, and looked out across the wasteland of ice.

It was flat, a vast plateau. Once, he knew, there had been rolling farmland here, hills and valleys, tree-clad hummocks, winding brooks cutting through the fields. He had seen the pictures of the world as it had been, so that he had some idea of what all those abstract concepts meant, those empty words, "hill" and "valley," "tree" and "brook." For more than three hundred years no New Yorker had seen hill or valley, tree or brook.

And none would now, Jim thought. The glacier, that great leveler, had drawn its white bulk over everything, smothering the world like a vast all-embracing beast. Here, in what had been the eastern part of the United States, the mile-thick ice sheet had created a uniform flatland. Jim knew that somewhere, thousands of miles to the west, the bare fangs of giant mountains stuck out high above the ice, but not here. The highest natural features in this part of the country were no more than fifteen hundred or two thousand feet high, and they were gone, buried without a trace, without causing so much as a bulge in the surface of the glacier.

When the ice finally retreated, the raw, wounded land would be revealed. The glacier, sluggishly

45

rolling down, had scraped topsoil and landmarks away, pushed them far to the south, deposited them in the terminal moraines, the great heaps of rubble that marked the southern border of the ice field. The land that one day would be freed from the glacier's grip would bear little resemblance to the thriving, populous zone of cities and towns that it had been, centuries ago.

And there, to the east—there the continent sloped off to meet the sea, or what had been the sea before the world grew cold. Was the Atlantic frozen? Would they be able to make the three-thousand-mile crossing safely, on pack ice? They would know soon enough, Jim thought. If the sleds worked, it would be only a short journey to the shore zone.

Footsteps crunched in the snow behind him. Jim turned.

"Hello, Carl. Big, isn't it?"

"Terrifying."

"Wish you had stayed in New York?"

"No," Carl said. "I'm glad I came."

Jim said, "Do you always do things on the spur of the moment like that, Carl?"

Carl chuckled. "Not really. It was just that —well, I'd been wondering for a long time: Was I doing anything important with my life? I mean, being a policeman. I hadn't taken any real training for any kind of profession, so I guess it was my own fault. But even though policemen are necessary in society, you don't get much feeling that you're *contributing* anything."

"I don't know," Jim said. "Somebody's got to maintain order."

"I suppose. But the job was boring me. I felt

restless. And then, after my father died, I had no family left, no ties in New York. Things were hatching in me. And then suddenly I knew what I wanted to do. To get out, to join your group, to see the upper world." Carl stamped his feet, rubbed his gloved hands together. Cold was turning his cheeks cherry red. "But tell me, Jim—"

"What?"

"Where are we going? What's this all about? Everything happened so fast." He grinned embarrassedly. "I really don't have any idea of what's up."

"We're going to London," Jim said. "We're going to cross the Atlantic ice."

"London? That's a million miles away!"

"Only three thousand, or so," Jim said.

"That's the same as a million, the way I look at it. But what's in London?"

"People. People like those in New York."

"Then why go to them?"

"Because New York doesn't want us," Jim said. "Mayor Hawkes and the Council tossed us out because we made radio contact with London. You know what radio is?"

Carl nodded.

"We talked to someone in London," Jim said. "He agreed with us that it was time to start coming out of the ground. Well, they got him. Roy thinks they killed him, and he's probably right. But we can't go on living in burrows. The ice is retreating."

"Is it?" Carl asked in surprise. "It doesn't look that way!"

"Maybe not here," Jim said. "But Dave says the worst is over. He's a meteorologist, you know. His

47

studies show that the temperature trend started to reverse itself about fifty years ago. The Earth is coming out of the dust cloud. Things are warming up. In another hundred or hundred and fifty years the ice may be gone from the United States."

"A hundred and fifty years! Then why should we be concerned?"

"Because," Jim said, "the time to start preparing is *now*. We've got to start exploring the surface again, to get the city people ready to live in the open. We have to plan ahead two or even three generations—just as they planned two generations ahead when they first built the underground cities. Only the Mayor didn't want to look that far ahead. If we left things up to him, nobody would ever come above ground again, not even if North America turned into the Garden of Eden!"

"I think I understand," Carl said. "Or maybe not. Anyway, I'm glad I'm here. It isn't everybody who gets to see what the world is like. Look at that moon! Look at it!"

Jim looked. He tingled in awe at the sight of that pockmarked round face, so blazing bright in the cold, black sky. Once, he knew, men had reached for the moon. Men had walked its dead surface. Mars, Venus—they had been reached, too. No one in New York knew what had happened to man's space dominion. Did the people of the tropical countries fly back and forth to the worlds of space every day? Or had the ice reached them too, finally, and choked off all thoughts but those of survival?

Jim turned his glance from the moon, back to the field of ice, to the white desert that stretched as far as the eye could see in every direction. He

48

scuffed at the snow, and watched it leap and scatter. And he kicked at the glacier, the obstinate mass of frozen water that had driven man from his domain.

"It's going to be quite a trip," he said quietly, as he and Carl trudged back to the tent.

It was Carl who first saw the sun.

"It's morning!" he yelled. "The sun is rising!"

Jim realized he had slept after all. He found himself lying in a corner of the tent, with somebody—Dom Hannon, it developed—sprawled across his legs. Getting to his feet, he found himself stiff and sore, every joint protesting against the cold. There was a general race for the exit from the tent.

"The sun," Dr. Barnes said quietly.

There wasn't much to see yet—a reddish-gold pinpoint of light, rising far to the east, just barely peeking above the white sheet of the glacier. But Jim felt choked as though a hand had grasped his throat. The sun!

"It's beautiful," he murmured.

It was rising with almost frightening speed. The whole upper lobe was above the horizon now; the color was changing from red to yellow, and in the clear blue sky scudded pink-bellied clouds of heart-numbing loveliness. A track of light seared along the ice plateau toward them like a runnel of golden, molten metal. The air was clear and cold, but not painfully so. Jim's cheeks and nose, which had suffered during the night, felt oddly stiff and brittle now, as though they might drop off at any moment, or as though they had *already* dropped off, but as he touched his skin he felt the blood

49

surge back into it. He was rapidly getting used to the cold weather.

Ted Callison was kneeling at the sleds, exposing the energy accumulators to the first rays of the sun. Higher it mounted, soaring into the sky. The clouds turned from pink to gold to pure white, and the glacier blazed so savagely that one could not look directly into the path of reflected light.

Now the world was clear to view. And the impression of the night was borne out: it was a plateau of cosmic size, stretching to the limits of eyesight.

"I hope they're having good breakfasts down there," Chet Farrington said. "But they can't be as hungry as I am!"

Jim looked down. Beneath his feet—a mile down, more than a mile—was the swarming bee-hive of New York! Eight hundred thousand people moving through the tunnels, on the way to the cafeterias for their first meal of the day. Standing here, all but alone on what could have been the world's first morning, Jim found it hard to believe that a noisy, bustling city lay below. Coming up from New York into the glacier world was like awakening from a lifetime-long dream—or like passing from reality to fantasy.

They ate—tinned provisions brought up from the world below. Synthetics. Hydroponic vegetables. Later on, Jim knew, they would have to start foraging for themselves. Was anything alive in this empty world? They could not eat ice, after all.

After breakfast, they broke camp and boarded the jetsleds. Ted Callison had studied the manuals, and told them that he figured the sleds had already soaked up enough solar energy to carry them a dozen miles before recharging. When the solar cells started to run down, they would have to halt and recharge for an hour or two. Eventually they would build up enough of a power backlog to drive the sleds all day, even with a few hours of clouds now and then.

They set off, two hours after sunrise. Eastward, into the sun.

The sleds functioned well, in spite of the centuries they had languished in storage. They moved slowly, no more than ten or fifteen miles an hour, but that was quite fast enough over the slippery ice. Jim, his father, Carl, and Dave Ellis rode in the lead sled; the other, with Ted Callison, Roy Veeder, Dom Hannon, and Chet Farrington aboard, followed.

Icy winds blew across the plateau, coming in from the east to slow them down. The travelers, bundled up so that only their faces were exposed to the elements, huddled down behind the curving shield of the sled's snout, peering sideways at the monotonous landscape.

Ice. Ice everywhere, and blue sky, and clouds of purest white, and the astounding fiery eye of the sun, climbing the sky and moving toward them even as they moved toward it. Not a tree, not a bird, not a sign of life to break the flat, white, barren sameness of it all.

"Is it going to be this way all the way to London?" Jim asked. "Three thousand miles of emptiness?"

"It'll be different when we reach the sea," Dr. Barnes promised. "But we'd better hope it's not too much different. If the sea isn't frozen over, we'll have to give up the idea of getting to London."

"What'll we do then, sir?" Carl wanted to know.

Dr. Barnes shrugged. "Head south, I guess. If we're lucky, the ice will already have retreated from Florida or Texas. If not, we'll just keep going into Mexico."

"Why don't we do that in the first place?" Dave Ellis put in. "Forget about London altogether?"

"No," Dr. Barnes said. "We've at least got to try to make contact with other underground cities. The people of the South aren't likely to be much friendlier toward us now than they were when the ice first came. We need to show a united front before we venture down to the lands that the ice never reached."

They fell silent. After a while, Jim said, "The sky is much clearer than I expected it to be. Where's the famous dust cloud that caused all the trouble?"

"It's there," Dave Ellis said. "Thinner than it was two-hundred years ago, probably, but it's there."

"Where?"

"Diffused in the atmosphere. One particle every few square feet, probably."

"And a little dust made the whole world freeze?" Carl asked.

Dave laughed. "It didn't take much to do the job," he said. "Just enough to screen off some of the sun's warmth—to drop the world's temperature by a few degrees. Once the process got started, it fed on itself. The colder it got, the more ice piled up; and the more ice piled up, the colder the seas and rivers got; and the colder they got, the

52

more snow fell. Round and round and round. And because it was so cold, more snow stuck than melted away. A few feet each year did the truck. But now it's going in reverse. The glaciers are *losing* a few feet every year. And as the Earth warms, the melting will get faster and faster."

"Where will all the water go?" Jim asked.

"Some of it will evaporate," Dave said. "There'll be heavy rains as a result. The dry parts of the world will get drenched as they haven't been in fifty thousand years. And a lot of the water will run into the oceans. Right now, the oceans are hundreds of feet below their normal sea levels. All that water is locked up, in the glaciers. The seas will rise tremendously as the glaciers melt."

"Won't the underground cities be drowned when the ice melts?" Carl asked.

Dave shook his head. "The cities are sealed. Besides, the water won't stay on the continental areas. It'll rush off down the slope to the ocean. And there'll be evaporation. Don't get the idea that everything will turn into a gigantic lake when the ice goes. It'll be gradual—a slow retreat."

Jim tried to picture a mile-thick glacier melting, and the water running off into the ocean. It defeated his imagination. It was hard for him even to imagine what an ocean could look like. Something like this frozen sea of ice, he figured, only wet, and moving with waves and currents. . . .

When they had covered eleven and a half miles, they stopped to recharge the accumulators. It was impossible to recognize any landmarks; so far as Jim could tell, they were right where they had

53

started, in the middle of an endless plateau of ice. But the sextant said they had traveled. And the sun was high overhead, now.

A few moments after they had halted, the first difference between this stopping place and the last became evident: they were not alone here.

There were shapes in the horizon. Dark, bulky figures were drawing near.

Ted Callison saw them first. He squinted into the blaze of light bouncing from the ice, and then grabbed hastily for the binoculars in Jim's knapsack.

"What do you see?" Jim asked.

"Things," Ted murmured. "Big ugly things."

"People?"

"No," he said. "Animals. Gigantic animals!"

By this time, nearly everyone had his field glasses out. Jim wrenched his own back from Ted, who fumbled in his knapsack for his rightful pair.

Jim gazed at the advancing creatures with amazement and mounting incredulity. It was hard to judge their size, since there were no trees or rocks to gauge them against, but they were big, at least half as high as a man. There were a dozen of them, shambling, hairy, four-legged creatures with sinister drooping snouts and a nest of complex bony-looking stuff sprouting from their heads.

Jim's pulse throbbed. In the underground city, there was neither room nor food for animals of any sort, not even dogs or cats. He had seen pictures of animals, just as he had seen pictures of trees and mountains, but the whole concept of living creatures who were not human left him a bit mystified.

54

Yet here they came, moving slowly over the ice, stooping now and then to lick the ground.

"What on earth are they?" Jim whispered.

"Could they be horses?" Dave Ellis asked. "Horses have four legs, I think."

"No," Chet Farrington said. "Horses don't have antlers—the things on their heads. These are some kind of moose. Or caribou, or elk. I don't remember the exact differences, but that's what these are."

"Dangerous?" Roy Veeder asked.

Chet shrugged. "I suppose they could be if we get them angry. Looks mostly like they're grazing on the ice. They aren't flesh-eaters."

*"Grazing?"* Jim asked. "On what?"

"Algae," Chet explained. "You studied hydroponics. You ought to know about algae."

"Sure," Jim said. "Microscopic plants. But living on the ice?"

"They've adapted to the cold. The moose lick them up. It's probably a full day's work for a moose to lick up enough algae to keep himself alive."

The creatures were grotesque, Jim thought. They were inhabitants of another world, the world of the glacier. He gripped the binoculars tightly, fascinated and repelled at the same time by the thick wooly fur, by the spindly legs with the wicked-looking hoofs, by the intricate convolutions sprouting from their heads. What was the word Chet had used? Antlers?

His nostrils, sensitive in the pure air, brought the smell of the beasts to him: rank, sickening.

"The wind's blowing toward us," Chet said.

"They don't smell us yet, and I guess they can't see us. But we'd better get our power torches ready. If they panic and run toward us, we might get trampled."

Ted Callison, who had been scanning the horizon, pointed suddenly toward the south.

"Here come some more of them!" he cried.

Everyone swung around to look. Jim saw only a dark line against the snow at first, but then the image resolved itself into—

"Those aren't animals coming now," Dr. Barnes said. "They're men. Hunters!"

_____ **5**

# *Nomads of the Ice World*

THERE WERE AT LEAST TWO DOZEN OF THEM, STALKING
the animals. They were still half a mile or more
away, but coming on steadily, a straggling line of
club-wielding men.

"Savages," Dr. Barnes said quietly. "Nomads of
the ice."

"Will they make trouble for us, Dad?"

"I don't know," the older man said. "Keep the
power torches handy, just in case."

The advancing hunters, though, showed no interest yet in the eight strangers to their territory.
All their attention was concentrated on the roam-

ing band of grazing beasts. Jim stared through his field glasses until his eyes throbbed with pain.

They were close enough to be seen in detail now. The hunters were short, brutish-looking men, squat and bulky, clad in animal skins and high leather leggings. Unkempt black hair tumbled to their shoulders. Some carried thick clubs, which Jim saw were fashioned not of wood but of the bones of some huge animal; others were armed with bows and arrows.

Keeping downwind of the grazers, the nomads began to fan out into a wide half-circle, surrounding them. Now and then one of the savages threw a curious look at the newcomers, but they kept their heads turned toward the animals.

The biggest, most majestic of the moose lifted his ponderous head. He had scented something! He pawed uneasily at the ice with his hoofs, took a few steps, turned to peer out of obviously short-sighted eyes at the attackers slowly creeping up on his band. The nomads were less than a hundred yards away now, and Jim was able at last to judge the true size of the beasts. They were enormous, seven and eight feet high at the shoulders.

One of the hunters was nocking an arrow. Thick muscles rippled and bulged as the string was drawn back. He let the arrow fly!

Straight on target it went, embedding itself in the throat of the lead moose! The superb creature reared and whirled, hurt but apparently not seriously crippled by the flimsy-looking shaft. The other animals began to mill, to grunt in distress as the circle of hunters closed in.

Suddenly the air was thick with arrows.

58

The moose were panicky, stampeding. Jim gasped as three of them burst through the circle, trampling down two hunters as though they were dolls. The two little men went sprawling. A rivulet of blood spread across the ice as the three beasts made good their escape.

The remaining moose, though, were still trapped in the now tight circle of hunters. Their hairy bodies bristled with the arrows lodged in them. One animal had fallen, an arrow in its eye, and lay writhing on the ice while two of the club-wielders pounded mercilessly at it. A second, battered to its knees, growled defiance and butted with its antlers at its assailants. A third, bleeding in a dozen places, still stood erect, trumpeting ear-splitting calls of anger over the ice.

The hunters closed upon them for the kill. Forgotten now were the other six animals, who were allowed to break through the circle and flee, despite their wounds. All three trapped moose were down, now, and clubs were flailing. The sight horrified Jim, but he forced himself to watch. He had never seen violent death before.

It was all over in a few minutes. Three great creatures lay dead on the ice. A dozen of the hunters went efficiently to work with bone knives, skinning the beasts, peeling off huge chunks of fat and meat and wrapping them in the animal hides for easy transportation.

Now, and only now, did the hunters deign to notice the eight strangers in their midst.

Three of the hunters strode over. They were short, Jim saw, no more than five feet tall, but their bodies were thick and hard-muscled, and they

59

showed no sign of distress over the exposure of their arms and faces to the cold. One was gray-haired and stubble-bearded, apparently the leader of the band. The other two were much younger. None of them looked at all friendly.

The old one said something. He spoke in short, sharp monosyllables, harsh grunting sounds that emerged as though each one cost him dearly.

Dr. Barnes replied, speaking clearly and loudly: "We come in peace. *Peace.*"

Again the monosyllabic grunts. The two younger hunters conferred in brusque whispers. The old chief stared malevolently at Dr. Barnes.

"Take this," Dr. Barnes said, and handed the power torch he was holding to Jim. He held out his hands, fingers upraised. "Peace," he repeated. "I carry no weapons. Peace! Friendship!"

Back came more incomprehensible words —higher in pitch now, more excited-sounding.

Dr. Barnes glanced at Dom Hannon. "Dom, does that language of theirs make any sense to you?"

The philologist shrugged. "It sounds as though it may have been English once. But the language has rotted away. There's nothing left of it but a few grunts. I can't pick up the sense of it."

Several other hunters detached themselves from the group dressing the kill, and strolled over. The scene began to look ugly. The hunters were sinister-looking little men, brutish and suspicious, and their bodies had the acrid smell of people among whom bathing is unknown.

"They must think we're trespassing on their hunting territory," Roy Veeder said. "He's probably warning us to get back to our own neighbor-hood.''

"If they try anything," Ted Callison muttered, "we'll let them have it with the torches!"

"No," Jim said. "They belong here and we don't. We've got no right to kill them!"

"Only in self-defense," Roy said. "Looks to me as if they're going to attack."

And, for a moment, it did appear that trouble was brewing. The parley was getting nowhere. Dr. Barnes and the nomad chief had given up the attempt to communicate through language, and were pantomiming, but even that was not creating much mutual understanding. The old chief had his knife out and was waving it through the air in a belligerent fashion, while Dr. Barnes smiled, spoke mildly, showed his empty hands, and pointed to himself and then onward toward the sea to indicate he was only passing through, not stay-ing to compete for hunting rights.

Meanwhile, the younger hunters were carrying on an independent—and heated—discussion of their own. It looked to Jim as if one of them were arguing for an immediate attack, the other one counseling patience.

All but five of the hunters had gathered round the parleyers now. The five were still busy with the kill. No one seemed at all interested in the two dead or dying men who had been trampled by the escaping animals.

Two of the youngest hunters were gripping their knives in an obviously menacing way. It seemed that in another moment violence might erupt between the two groups. Dr. Barnes was grimly acting out every kind of charade that he thought might pacify the hunters, but he clearly did not appear to be getting through.

Suddenly he turned. "Carl, do you have police medic training?"

"Yes, sir. First aid, at least."

"All right. Get your medic kit and come on with me. You too, Jim. Keep that power torch handy, just in case they misunderstand."

Jim and Carl followed Dr. Barnes across the ice to where the fallen hunters lay. A stir ran through the band of nomads, but they remained gathered together, muttering to one another.

Dr. Barnes knelt by the side of one hunter. The fallen man wasn't a pretty sight. Flying hoofs had crashed into him and knocked him down, other hoofs had trampled across his skull. His face was nothing but a bloody smear. His chest was caved in.

"Nothing we can do for him, poor devil," Dr. Barnes muttered. "Let's see about the other one."

The second man was still alive. His fur jacket was half ripped off, and Jim could see the ugly gouge in his chest where a passing moose had kicked him. The hairy, dirty skin was purple and swollen around the wound. He had been kicked in several other places, too, and the skin had been broken, but he did not seem really badly hurt.

Carl opened the medic kit and took out retractors and a sterilizer. He worked briskly and efficiently; he was no doctor, but medical equipment had been refined to the point where anyone with a little first-aid training could take care of even serious injuries. Dr. Barnes moved the wounded man into position while Carl drew back the edges of the big gash with the retractors and passed the sterilizer the length of the cut. A quick hum, a flash of light, and the danger of infection was past.

Carl took a flesh-sealer from the little medic kit. Tiny metal claws seized the ragged edges of the wound, drew them together.

"He's going to have a pretty ugly scar," Carl said apologetically. "I'm not very good at matching the tissues yet, I'm afraid."

"Don't let it worry you," Dr. Barnes said. "They were going to leave him for dead."

"They're coming over to have a look," Jim said uneasily. "The whole bunch of them. They look ugly."

"Just go on working, Carl," Dr. Barnes said quietly. He glanced up at Jim. "Let them come within about six feet of us, but no closer. And stay cool."

Jim nodded. He watched the nomads crowd round, and held the power torch in readiness, though without aiming it. The nomads seemed awed by the instruments Carl was using, and they kept their distance, their mood changing from one of menace to one of uncertainty and fear.

Carl worked methodically, closing the wound, sealing it with the heat-and-pressure device that had replaced surgical stitches centuries before. When he was finished, a ragged red line ran down the man's chest—but the wound was closed.

"Go on," Dr. Barnes said. "Let's get the other cuts now."

In a matter of minutes, the injured hunter's wounds were rendered aseptic and sealed. The man stirred. His eyes opened, and he looked at his saviors in dull incomprehension. He lifted a shaky hand, touched it to the rough patch of sterile plastispray covering the wound on his chest. Then he looked at his companions and said something to them. They answered with hoots of amazement. The injured man tried to get to his feet, rose as far as his knees, halted there, dizzy, swaying. Two of the hunters started forward to help him, then hesitated until Carl and Dr. Barnes stepped back.

The injured man rose, leaning against them, and took a few hobbling steps. A moment later, every hunter had his knife drawn!

Jim leveled the power torch, ready to wipe out the whole band if he had to. But he relaxed as he saw what the nomads were doing.

They were tossing their knives down at Carl's feet!

Carl grinned in amazement and surprise as each of the hunters, in turn, added his bone knife to the heap, then withdrew and sank to his knees in the snow. The last to pay homage was the grizzled old chief himself. He came forward almost grudgingly, flipped his knife onto the pile, and dropped in obeisance.

"I think you've just become chief of the tribe, Carl," Jim said with a laugh.

Carl turned to Dr. Barnes. "What do I do now?"

"Pick up the chief's knife. Hand it back to him."

Carl did so. The chief, still kneeling, stared blankly at the crude bone knife as Carl offered it, butt first. He did not seem to understand at all. Carl pressed the knife into his hand, and in sudden inspiration touched the old man's shoulder, as if giving a blessing. Then he stepped back.

The chief rose, sheathing the knife, and for the

first time broke into a broad smile, baring the stubs of worn yellow teeth.

After that everything was simple. The gulf in communication that had existed was magically bridged. Now, Dr. Barnes's pantomiming got across, as was shown by the smiles and the excited chatter of the hunting folk. Dr. Barnes pointed to himself, to the other seven city people, and then toward the sea. The nomad chief nodded. With his knife, he drew a line in the snow, indicated their present location by tapping his chest and then the ground, and sketched out a second line running from that point to the other line. He repeated it several times.

"What's he trying to tell us?" Jim asked.

"I think he's saying that we can have safe conduct as far as his territory reaches," Dr. Barnes said. "Another few miles, at any rate."

The crisis was past. The injured hunter, still shaky but able to move around, had rejoined his comrades. Jim watched as they cut away a slab of ice and buried their dead fellow in the glacier, heaping snow to hide his body.

Then a new crisis developed—far less menacing than the last one, but just as perplexing. The man who had been wounded sought out Carl, carrying in his hands a raw gobbet of moose meat! He held the great bloody chunk of flesh out toward his savior.

Carl took the meat, but held it gingerly, looking at it with barely concealed disgust.

"What am I supposed to do with it?" he asked.

"Eat it," Dr. Barnes said. "It's a friendship offering."

65

"*Eat* it? *Raw?*"

"He'll take offense otherwise," Dr. Barnes said.

Carl shuddered, and Jim had to turn away, laughing at the husky ex-policeman's plight. Carl took a bit of the red meat, grimaced, gulped.

A moment later, Jim was laughing out of the other side of his mouth as a slimy hunk of meat was pressed into *his* hands, too. The nomads were showing their friendship in the only way they knew how, by offering food, and one at a time they were coming forward to give meat to the newcomers.

The eight city men forced back their qualms and ate, for the sake of peace. Even Chet, with his famous appetite, looked uneasy. Jim took a bite, retched, gagged, and tensed every muscle to keep the meat down. The idea of eating flesh, raw flesh, sickened him. There were no meat animals in the underground city. Men got their protein in other ways. And to stand here, in thirty-degree weather, munching on the raw flesh of an animal that had been alive half an hour before . . .

"Eat," Dr. Barnes commanded, as they hesitated after a few bites.

Jim ate. Carl ate. They all ate, pointing at each other's blood-smeared jowls, making a grim joke out of the ceremony of friendship.

Once the first queasiness was past, Jim discovered to his surprise that he rather liked the taste of the meat. Not the texture of it—it was too slick, too wet—but the gamy taste appealed to him. Probably the meat tasted quite delectable when cooked. He ate as much as he could hold, and then, when he felt he could take no more, he quietly slipped the rest into a sleeve of his parka when no hunter was looking, and stooped to wash the moose blood from his gloves and face with snow.

The hunters had all repossessed their knives by this time, and had gone back to their prey to finish stripping and preparing the animals for transportation back to wherever their encampment might be. The city men, looking pale and a little wobbly, exchanged feeble grins as their digestive systems went to work on their unfamiliar fare.

"That wasn't so bad, was it?" Dr. Barnes asked.

"Better than having a fight, I guess," Jim said. "Only the next time, maybe we can cook the meat."

"I rather like it this way," Ted Callison remarked.

Dave Ellis, the meteorologist, glared at him. "You *would*," he grumbled. "Savage!"

Callison took no offense. "You wait, paleface," he said. "By and by we get hungry again, run out of moose meat. I eat meteorologist meat! Raw!"

Everyone laughed—all but Dave. Even the hunters, busy with their gory work, looked up and joined the general chorus of laughter.

Jim looked toward them. "Who do you think they are, Dad?"

"Survivors," Dr. Barnes said. "Descendants of people who didn't go underground. They waited out the worst of the cold somewhere south of here, then came back when things got a little better."

"But there's nothing to live on up here!" Jim said.

"No? There's moose, at least. And probably plenty of other game, too. It must be a hard life, but they seem to have survived for centuries this way. Men can adapt to almost any kind of conditions, Jim. Even before the glaciers came, there were men who lived in the Arctic in conditions very much like these. Eskimos. They lived there voluntarily, and made a good life out of it. It was the only life they knew.''

"Are these men Eskimos?" Carl asked.

Dr. Barnes shook his head. "The Eskimos were Asiatics. These men are of our own race. They've adapted to the cold, but they're descended from the same kind of people we are.''

"Why couldn't we understand their language, then?" Roy Veeder wanted to know.

Dom Hannon said, "Because we've been living in isolation for centuries, and they've been up here. Languages change. They've boiled theirs down to a few syllables. Remember how much trouble we had understanding the Londoners? And they've lived the same kind of life we have. These nomads don't need all our fancy words. They've scrapped every excess sound.''

The hunters were nearly finished with their chores. Blood stained a wide area of the ice, animal blood, and the picked carcasses of the dead moose looked weirdly naked. Almost everything useful had been carved away and neatly packed up in skin for the trek back to their encampment, probably many miles away across the forbidding glacier.

All this while the sled accumulators had been charging themselves, too. It was time for the eight voyagers to be moving along.

They boarded the sleds. The nomads, still friendly, tried to climb aboard also, but Carl held up his hand to keep them back, and they obeyed.

The sleds started. As they began to glide off across the ice, the hunters followed, their eyes wide at the sight of this new wonder of men moving without exerting themselves. Jim settled down, feeling his stomach rebelling once again at the lunch it had had to endure. The motion of the sled didn't help matters any. He gulped hard, clenched his jaws.

Carl laughed. "Still hungry, Jim?"

"Very funny," Jim growled. He took a deep breath, and the spasm passed. Looking back, he saw the nomad hunters trekking along behind the sled, grinning and waving as the city people gradually drew away from them.

In a little while, they were lost to sight. The world seemed empty once again. There was nothing but whiteness, stretching off toward the distant horizon.

# 6

## *To the Sea!*

THEY SAW NO MORE NOMADS THAT AFTERNOON. THE sleds glided on, always eastward over the endless ice plateau, and the sun passed them and began to dip toward the westward horizon. A late-afternoon chill swept down on them. The temperature began to drop, falling sharply almost from minute to minute. When they had traveled another twenty miles, the sun was nearly down, and it was time to halt for the night.

Jim, Carl, and Ted Callison broke out the tents. Chet and Roy lit a fire, feeding it with synthetic-fuel pellets. Dom Hannon and Dave Ellis began to open food containers for dinner, while Dr. Barnes patrolled the area, power torch in hand, as though he expected an attack any moment.

They ate in silence. The wind was biting now, and the temperature was getting near the zero mark, though it was still early in the evening. The moon was up, even bigger and more brilliant than the night before. In the unearthly silence of the ice field, where the only sounds were the howling of the wind and the crunch of a footfall against crisp snow, all the world seemed locked in an eternal freeze.

And then, across the flat wasteland, came the bloodchilling wails of hungry beasts.

"Listen," Jim whispered.

"It's the wind," Dave Ellis said.

"No. No, it's not!"

Ted Callison, whose eyes were the sharpest among them, had his field glasses out. As he had earlier that day, he spied animals coming toward them. But not grazing animals, this time.

"They look like dogs," he said. He hefted his power torch. "Big dogs. A whole pack of them!"

"Wolves," Chet muttered. "They've seen the fire, and they're coming to eat."

The pack was clearly visible in the moonlight now: fifteen, perhaps twenty long, lean shapes, pattering across the ice, baying as they came. Through his binoculars, Jim could see the curling pink tongues, the slavering jaws. Who said the glacier world was an empty one, he wondered? Moose—hunters—now a pack of hungry wolves . . .

"Push the sleds together!" Ted Callison yelled. "Make a barricade!"

They huddled behind the sleds. Jim, his father,

Ted, and Roy held the four power torches, and crouched in readiness, while the other four men armed themselves with ice hatchets, knives, anything that might protect them in case the wolves burst through the barricade. The power torches had an effective range of only some twenty or thirty feet, which meant the wolves would have to be allowed to come quite close before firing.

Onward they came. But their steady lope broke into a suspicious slink as they came within close range of the camp. They had been running in tight formation; now they separated and fanned out over the ice.

"Ugly devils," Ted murmured.

Jim nodded, keeping his finger close to the stud of the torch. The wolves looked enormous, bigger than a man, their yellow eyes gleaming by the light of the fire, their sides hollow, their shanks flat. Snarling, growling, barking, they closed in on the encampment, wary but obviously unafraid.

Half a dozen of the brutes were within torch range now.

"Let 'em have it!" Dr. Barnes shouted.

Jim rammed the stud forward, and felt the blood surge in his veins as the beam of light blazed forth to envelop one fang-toothed attacker. He switched the torch off rapidly. The wolf was gone; two severed legs that had not been in the torch's blasting field lay horridly in a puddle of melted ice, and a smell of singed fur drifted through the air.

But there was no time now, for sensations of either triumph or revulsion. The wolves were charging desperately! Dr. Barnes brought down one, and Ted two with two quick blasts, but one of the others somehow sidestepped a destructive bolt

72

and leaped with terrifying grace, arching upward and over the barrier. Roy swung his torch upward and fired while the wolf was still in mid-leap. The creature seemed to disintegrate as the bolt took it, and the air sizzled and crackled for a moment, eddying in ragged currents around the place where the wolf had been.

Jim's torch claimed a second victim, and a third, but then he saw two wolves come soaring over the barricade simultaneously, and there was no way to fire without blasting away half of one sled. The nearer of the snarling monsters came right at Jim; he smelled the wolf-stink of it, stared right into the frightful eyes. Unable to fire the torch, he swung it around, bashed it butt end first into the wolf's snout.

The impact of the blow sent the wolf reeling back, blood dripping, broken fangs dropping to the ice. It circled Jim, ready for a second spring, but this time drew itself far enough away from the sled so that he could take a shot at it. The torch turned it to ash even as it readied itself to rip Jim's throat out.

The other wolf had gone for Chet. His only defense was a hatchet, which he swung with telling effect as the monster leaped. He caught the wolf's left shoulder, and bright blood fountained. But the hatchet went skittering away, and a moment later Chet was sprawling on the ice behind the sled, the wolf covering him and going for his throat.

Jim shouted and plunged forward, handing his power torch to Dave Ellis. Chet was struggling against the savage creature, holding the snapping jaws away from him with all the strength in his long, muscle-corded arms. Drawing his hunting knife, Jim threw himself down, the blade digging deep. The wolf shivered convulsively as Jim dragged the knife through its hairy belly, and rolled to one side. Chet scrambled free, and they both leaped back.

"I've got him!" Dr. Barnes roared, and fired. The wolf died in a blaze of nuclear fury.

"You all right?" Jim asked.

Chet nodded. "Just some claw scratches."

Turning, Jim saw Dave Ellis blazing away with the torch Jim had given him. The meteorologist's timidity seemed forgotten in the excitement of battle. Two wolves at once were coming at Dave, and he bellowed at them, a primordial, spine-shivering cry of fury and hatred, and cut them down in quick order. Seeing that Dave was taking good care of himself, Jim gripped his knife and looked to see where he could be useful.

But everything was under control. A single wolf remained, growling viciously on the far side of the sleds, but coming no closer. Ted Callison dispatched the creature with a quick bleep of light, and the attack was over.

Steam rose from the ice. The repeated blasts of the power torch had melted small lakes on both sides of the barricade, but they were already beginning to refreeze at the edges. Fragments of wolf lay everywhere. The stink of destruction clawed at Jim's nostrils. There was fresh blood on his gloves, not moose blood this time but wolf blood, and he trembled a little as he remembered how it had felt to thrust the gleaming blade deep within the belly of a living creature.

Dr. Barnes, still holding his power torch, inspected them.

"Everyone okay? Jim? Chet?"

"I'm a little scratched," Chet reported.

"Take care of him, will you, Carl?" Dr. Barnes said. He mounted one of the sleds and looked around. "No more in sight. But we'd better keep watch through the night. Three-hour shifts, I guess. Let's clean up the mess first."

Chet laughed. "It's too bad we wasted those wolves," he said. "The meat might have been useful later on."

"I'd rather eat moose," Jim said. "These fellows were all tooth and claw and muscle."

They cleaned up, fastidiously heaping the remains of the dead wolf pack together and covering the refuse with snow. Then they settled in for the night. Dr. Barnes and Ted Callison drew the first watch shift together.

Jim huddled down in the tent. He heard howls from without, and told himself that it was just the howling of the wind. He was fiercely tired. It had been a long, hard day—a day that seemed to have lasted years.

But they had met challenges out here in this forbidding world of ice, and they had responded to them, had triumphed. What more could they ask? He had eaten raw meat today, and he had killed wild beasts. In a single day, he thought, the Jim Barnes whose skin he had worn for seventeen years had changed almost beyond recognition. It was well, he told himself. He was adapting to this rugged new life. He was adapting.

Waking was a struggle. Jim would rather have

75

fought a dozen wolves barehanded than to have come up out of sleep. But the hand that gripped his shoulder shook mercilessly, and finally he pried his bleary eyes open and saw Dave Ellis crouched over him.

"Your shift," he said. "Wake up!"

It was nearly dawn. The night had passed rapidly and uneventfully. Jim and Carl, armed with torches just in case, sat shivering in the bitter cold while their comrades slept. Somewhere, twenty or thirty miles behind them and more than a mile straight down, New York's eight hundred thousand people slumbered warm and safe in their beds. Jim did not envy them, though. Better to shiver blue-lipped up here, wolves and nomads and all, than to hide like a worm in the ground!

The moon slipped from sight. The sky turned from black to iron-gray, then blued as the day dawned. The first pink streaks of morning stained the sky, and the sun rose, a beacon in the east, beckoning to them to continue their journey.

The sleepers were up soon after sunrise. They had a light breakfast, and while they waited for the jet's accumulators to charge themselves, Ted Callison broke out the radio and started to toy with it.

"What are you doing?" Chet asked him.

"Calling London," Ted answered. "We might as well let them know we're coming."

But there was no response. Ted tried channel after channel, and nothing came in but the dry crackle of static, and then it was time to move on.

The day was colder than yesterday had been. Clouds hid the sun half the time, and a sharp wind came slicing down from the north. The temperature never got above fifteen degrees. The monotony of the journey was broken only twice during the day: in the morning, a solitary wolf loped past them, gave them a startled look, and streaked out of sight. Late that day, as they neared the end of their travel for the afternoon, they came upon the remains of a nomad encampment. Five domeshaped houses had been built of blocks of ice—"igloos," Dr. Barnes called them—and within were a few gnawed animal bones, some discarded ropes made of wolf sinew, and a broken knife. Of the igloo-builders themselves, there was no sign, and from the looks of things the camp had been abandoned some weeks back.

The next day it snowed. Light, powdery flakes came spiraling down out of the gray sky. The sight was a beautiful one, but it was no fun having the snow drifting into your face all morning, Jim decided. And the sunless day slowed them, since the sleds could not charge and power soon ran short. They had to halt after having gone only fifteen miles. The snow stopped late in the afternoon. Jim, Carl, and Dom Hannon amused themselves by trying to build an igloo, but the job defeated them. Arranging the foundation blocks was easy enough, but getting the dome to curve properly proved to be no task for amateur architects.

Ted Callison watched them, smiling sardonically. "You ought to be able to do a better job than that," he told them. "If those illiterate, skin-wearing nomads can build these things, why can't you intelligent New Yorkers do it?"

"Maybe because we're intelligent New Yorkers," Dom Hannon retorted. "Instead of living out here in the ice and learning how, our ancestors were keeping warm down below."

"Why don't you show us how to do it, Ted?" Carl invited. "They tell me you're an Indian, so you ought to know."

"Indians aren't Eskimos," Ted said thinly. "My people lived in log cabins."

"I thought Indians lived in wigwams," Jim said. Ted favored him with a look of vast scorn. "Where did *you* study your ancient history? Some Indians lived in wigwams, some lived in wooden cabins, some lived in pits in the ground, and some lived in apartment houses made of brick."

"And some lived in igloos," Carl added.

"Those were Eskimos!" Ted said, and made a face as he saw he was once again being teased. "Oh, what's the use! Here, let me show you children how to build your little igloo."

But he had no better luck than they had. After fifteen minutes of trying to put a dome on the igloo, he gave up and walked away, his normally ruddy cheeks red with cold and redder still from embarrassment. As he disappeared into the tent, Jim heard him exclaim something about, "Wrong kind of foundation, that's the trouble!"

Once again, they guarded themselves in shifts during the night, but no wolves came to harass them this time. Jim had been lucky the first night, drawing the dawn shift so that he could sleep most of the night without interruption, but the fates were against him tonight. He and Dom Hannon picked short straws and had to take the middle shift, which meant sleeping a few hours, then being awakened to stand sentry, and back to sleep —if possible—afterward.

It was an uneventful night. Jim began to get the picture of the ice-world as being populated by sparse groups of nomads, tribes that gave each other plenty of elbowroom, and by roaming bands of animals whose numbers were not very great, since the land could not support them. The wolves probably fed on the moose, and the moose, Chet had told them, fed on the tiny green and red plants that miraculously grew right on the surface of the ice, and the hunters fed on the moose and most likely on the wolves as well. There did not seem to be any birds, and Jim found that disappointing. The idea that animals actually could fly had always seemed fantastic to him when he read about it in books dealing with life of the pre-Ice Age, and he had hoped to see birds in flight when he left New York. But there were none here, at least not so far as any of them had yet seen.

The next day was warm, almost summery compared with the last two. The sun was bright in the clear blue sky, and the temperature climbed well above freezing, so that most of yesterday's snow melted and turned to slush that went splashing outward as the runners of the sled cut through it. They made good time, traveling almost forty miles before they had to stop to recharge. In their three days so far, they had covered only eighty miles, and at that rate it would take ages to reach London. But the sleds were accumulating power; each sunny day, they increased the backlog, storing away more energy than they actually used for travel, so that in a few days more they would be able to use the sleds eight to ten hours at a stretch, on a bright day, and still have nearly as much power in storage as when they started.

79

On the fourth morning, they spied a distant encampment of nomads, far out to the south —dark dots on the horizon, nothing more. It might have been a herd of moose or a pack of wolves, but that smoke could plainly be seen rising to the sky. So the nomads had fire—some of them, at least.

"What do they use for fuel?" Jim asked. "There's no wood here, no coal—"

"They must burn animal oils," Ted Callison suggested.

It struck Jim as an eerie life these people must lead—without metal, without real fuel, without books, without plastics, without synthetics. Yet they survived. The glaciers had covered the United States for century upon century, and still the stubborn bands of huntsmen endured. Of course, as his father had said, they had probably not been in the area all along. During the worst part of the Ice Age, some two hundred years back, when the sun scarcely shone and the temperature rarely rose as high as zero, not even these hardy wanderers could have survived. They must have gone south and then wandered north fifty or a hundred years ago, perhaps forced into the colder regions by unfriendly peoples living in the relatively warm parts of the world.

As they ventured onward during the day, Jim began to notice something odd happening to the glacier over which they were traveling. It appeared to be sloping, ever so gently, toward the east.

He said nothing about it for a while, for he was not certain that he really saw what he thought he was seeing. Possibly it was only some trick of perspective, or some folly of his eyes, brought on by staring too intently at empty white wastelands. Still, the impression persisted, and as he looked backward over the miles they had traveled, he became certain that the plateau really *was* dipping, that they were moving down the side of a very gentle incline.

When they halted to eat, late in the day, he decided to ask his father about it. Dr. Barnes had left the sled and had walked perhaps fifty feet away, and stood by himself, a tall, spindly figure outlined sharply against the white backdrop. He was staring off toward the distance, frozen in the deepest concentration, and for a moment Jim was uncertain about disturbing him.

"Dad?" he said finally.

"What is it, Jim?"

"I was wondering," Jim said, pointing back up the slope. "Isn't the ice field dropping? Is it just an optical illusion, or have we been going downhill all day?"

Dr. Barnes grinned and shook his head. "It's no illusion. We're heading down the eastern face of the glacier now. Down toward the sea. And we're almost to it."

"Really?"

Dr. Barnes stretched one long arm off toward the east. "Right down there," he said. "We'll reach it tomorrow, I figure. We're nearing the continental shelf, and that drops right down into the Atlantic."

Jim stared. All he could see was whiteness—and the plain in front of them seemed almost level.

Almost.

But yet it sloped. The glacier was tailing off. It held sway only over the land. Out there in the

81

whiteness somewhere the land came to an end, and the broad Atlantic—frozen, as white as the land—waited for them.

The sea! The all-but-endless sea!

And beyond it, London. Jim felt like a Columbus going the wrong way. Doggedly, desperately, against all the odds, men from the New World had set out to rediscover Europe. Turning, he looked back at the setting sun, reddening the ice that lay to the westward, and a cold, shaking thrill gripped his nerves and muscles. He yearned for it to be tomorrow, so that they could break camp and move on, onward toward the sea!

## _____ 7

## *A Ring of Spears*

MORNING WAS BRIGHT AND CLEAR—THE SECOND FINE
day in a row, as the ice-world turned toward
summer. The voyagers were on the move early,
within an hour of dawn. The ice glittered gold as
they sped eastward.

There was no mistaking the slope now. The
glacier dropped off toward sea level—the *old* sea
level—and lay in a sheet no more than a few
hundred feet thick over what had once been a shelf
of submerged land. They had already passed the
old shore line, and perhaps even over the site of old
New York, its proud skyscrapers still strangled in

the grip of the ice, its cloud-stabbing towers buried thousands of feet down.

Beyond lay the sea, itself frozen, distinguishable from the glacier only by its lower altitude. The new sea level was probably several hundred feet below the old, since so much water lay locked in glaciers, and a relatively thin crust of ice lay over the surface of the ocean. Just how sturdy that crust of ice would prove to be was a matter to be tested when the proper time came, a day or two hence.

They headed down the slope.

When they had traveled ten miles, it became apparent that a nomad camp lay squarely in their path. Dark shapes moved on the horizon, and sharp-eyed Ted Callison reported that he saw at least a dozen igloos.

"All right," Dr. Barnes said. "We'll change course a little and avoid them."

"That'll waste time," Ted argued.

"Can't be helped. It'll waste more time if we have to stop and parley with the nomads. Let's cut to the north and go around them."

The sleds angled northward. But moments later it appeared that the maneuver was pointless. The nomads were breaking camp! They were on the move, too—heading northward as if to intercept the sleds.

"Looks as if they're trying to cut us off," Chet Farrington said. "There must be a hundred of them."

Dr. Barnes nodded unhappily. "We're trespassing on their territory, I guess."

"If we cut farther north—" Jim suggested.

"No, Jim. They'll only follow us all over the

place. And we've got to stop for recharging soon anyway. I guess we'll just have to deal with them."

The party changed course again, heading due eastward now, straight into the nomad line. As they drew nearer, it could be seen that this band was considerably larger than the hunting party they had met a few days earlier. Not only that, but they were better equipped, dressed in well-made leather clothes whose careful tailoring indicated considerable skill.

They had been spread out in a thin line, stretching from north to south in the path of the sleds. Now the glacier dwellers gathered together, forming a tight semicircle whose ends curved toward the city people. An ominous muttering could be heard, and as the sleds approached within a few hundred feet, the tribesmen suddenly couched their weapons in open sign of hostility: not clubs or bone knives, this time, but long, wicked-looking bone-tipped spears.

"Somehow I get the feeling they aren't going to be as friendly as the last bunch," Dave Ellis said.

Jim laughed and looked at Carl. "Better get your medic kit ready," he said. But he did not feel very amused at the situation.

The sleds halted. Dr. Barnes, tight-lipped and tense-looking, stepped from the lead sled and went forward to parley. Jim took a firm grip on a power torch. His father looked so terribly vulnerable, standing there alone in the open space between the two groups. His long, lean figure was rock-steady, but who knew what uneasiness he felt? A single accurate cast of one of those spears, and . . .

Dr. Barnes said, that amazingly deep booming

voice of his coming resonantly out of his narrow chest, "We mean no harm. We come in peace."

A figure stepped out of the semicircle. It was that of a thick-bodied, powerful-looking man of middle years, whose glossy, curling black beard hung almost to the middle of his barrel of a chest. His voice matched Dr. Barnes's in deepness—and, Jim realized in wonder, his words could be understood!

"What folk be ye?" he demanded.

"Folk from far away," Dr. Barnes replied. "We come from the sunset land. We go toward the sunrise."

"Ye be trespassers here!" came the cold, somber reply. "This be Dooney turf!"

"We will not stay," Dr. Barnes said. "Nor will we hunt here. We ask leave to pass through Dooney turf on our way to the sunrise land."

"Pay ye the toll, then!"

"Which is?"

The Dooney chieftain smiled craftily. His dark, glittering eyes raked the faces of the seven city men waiting in the sleds. After a long moment of silence he said, "The toll be—the life of one of your warriors!"

Dr. Barnes seemed to stiffen. Jim gasped, and clasped his fist so tightly his nails scratched deep into his palm. The Dooney chieftain spoke in a thick voice, and with a barbarous accent, but there was no mistaking the meaning of his words. The toll for passing through Dooney turf—one life!

"No," Dr. Barnes said. "Such a toll we will not pay."

"Then ye do not pass!"

"The savage," Dave Ellis murmured. "The dirty,

foul-smelling, greasy-haired savage! Why does he have to make trouble for us? What would it cost him to let us through?"

"Pride," Jim said. "This strip of ice is his kingdom. And he's going to make us pay to get through!"

Dr. Barnes said, his tone softer now, "Why take a life? We can offer other toll."

"A life!" the Dooney chief rumbled. "No else!"

"What good is a dead man?" Dr. Barnes asked. "He can do no labor for you. He can slay no game. There is not even meat enough on a dead man's bones to feed your people for a day. Let us give you something else, then." Dr. Barnes reached to his belt and drew out his keen hunting knife. The shining blade gleamed mirror-bright in the midday sun. "Look!" he shouted. "A knife that cuts everything!" He drew up his left arm and slashed the blade through the outer lining of his jacket sleeve. "See? It cuts like fire! We will give you knives!"

The Dooney leader spat contemptuously. "We have knives, stranger. What good be your knives? They be no better than our!"

"A hatchet, then." Turning, Dr. Barnes beckoned toward the sled. Jim found one of the ice axes and bore it to his father, who hefted it, lifted it high, brought it down resoundingly into the floor of ice. Chips sprayed; he hacked again and again, and in moments was able to lift a thick slab of ice.

It made an impression on the Dooney folk. The spearsman, obviously amazed by the speed with which the axe had cut free the slab, as compared with the time it took for them to slice out a block of ice with their knives of bone, jabbed one another in the ribs, and muttered whispers of awe. Only the chief remained impassive. His scowl deepened.

Dr. Barnes held forth the axe. "Here," he said. "Take this as your toll."

"No. Our toll be one life. Else ye go back where you came. Ye do not pass!"

For an ugly moment of silence the two leaders confronted each other. Then Dr. Barnes shrugged and stepped back, his shoulders slumping. He returned to the sleds.

"It's hopeless," he said. "He's determined to show us what a big man he is. Ted, how are the accumulators doing?"

"We could use another half hour of charging."

"Well, we'll get it somewhere else. Let's continue onward," Dr. Barnes said. "If we have to, we'll just head north until we're out of Dooney territory —even if it takes us all week."

He climbed back into the lead sled. But the Dooney folk were not minded to give up their demands so easily, it seemed. They moved forward, uncertainly, in a ragged line, until they were only a dozen yards from the sleds. The chief shouted a hoarse, guttural command.

Suddenly the ragged line shaped up in tight formation. The Dooney warriors assembled themselves into a circle, completely surrounding the sleds.

The eight wanderers stared with dismay at a ring of spears!

"Start the sleds," Dr. Barnes ordered quietly. "Dave, give me that power torch. Jim, Ted, Roy —keep your torches ready, but don't use them unless there's an attack."

88

Jim nodded. He tried to imitate his father's calmness, but this did not strike him as a situation for calmness at all. Fighting off a hundred armed and hostile barbarians was not the same thing as slaughtering twenty hungry wolves. These were human beings, these men with spears, and Jim shivered at the thought that in a few moments he might be called upon to blast the life out of them with the power torch. To take any life ran powerfully against his beliefs. But to take *human* life—!

It could be self-defense, he told himself. But even that had a hollow, hollow ring.

The sled motors whirred. The ring of spears bristled as the warriors went tense. Their faces showed a mingling of fear and defiance, always a bad combination.

"Let's go," Dr. Barnes said. "Due east. Maybe they'll break ranks if we start to run them down."

The sleds glided forward at a crawl, moving no faster than two or three miles an hour. The warriors backed up, but held their formation, keeping their tight ring around the sleds even as they moved.

Jim eyed the spearsmen uneasily. Power torches against bone-tipped spears did not seem like much of a contest—except that there were only four torches, and more than a hundred spears. If the Dooney folk attacked, the torches might take thirty or forty lives in the first moments of combat—but, trapped as the eight men were within the ring of spears, they could not hope to withstand the furious onslaught of the survivors.

The chieftain's jaws were working, but he was saying nothing. The sleds rolled forward. Now they

89

were no more than a dozen feet from the eastern curve of the ring. The chief himself stood there, eyes blazing.

"Stop!" he cried. "Toll be paid or ye die!"

Dr. Barnes lifted the power torch. Was he going to gun the chief down, Jim thought? Murder him in cold blood and perhaps touch off a massacre?

"Jim, take your cap," he said. "Fling it high in the air, straight overhead, high as you can. Ted, Dave, get ready to open the sleds to full throttle."

Jim understood. He pushed back his hood, removed his cap, cocked his arm, tossed it high —thirty, forty feet into the air. The eyes of the Dooney warriors followed it.

Dr. Barnes aimed and fired.

The power torch spurted a globe of light. The dropping hat fell into it. . . .

And then light and hat winked out of existence.

The Dooney warriors screamed like women at the terrifying sight. Sudden destruction—a hand that could reach into the sky and destroy—they had never seen anything like it! Panic swept them.

"Full speed ahead!" Dr. Barnes shouted.

The spearsmen were fleeing, the ring breaking up, fur-clad warriors scrambling helter-skelter away from the frightening beings from the sunset land. Only the Dooney chieftain himself stood his ground, roaring like an enraged bull, bellowing to his men to return to formation, thundering at them to strike the invaders dead.

The sleds rolled toward him. With a sudden frenzied cry of anger and frustration, the barbarian chieftain hurled his spear into one of the sleds, and an instant later himself came leaping over the runners and threw himself upon Dr. Barnes!

90

Jim went into action without pausing to think. In the underground city, he had painstakingly learned how to make the most of his natural endowments, how to focus his strength for maximum effort. *Judo*, it was called, the technique of defense through body leverage. It had been born, so it was said, in a country called Japan, far to the west. Jim knew nothing of Japan, but he knew judo well, and now he employed his knowledge against the Dooney chieftain. He rose and lunged forward, grabbing the powerful old man by his shoulders and pulling him away from his father's much lighter form. There was no question of using power torches in the cramped confines of the sled, and no time to draw a knife. Jim tugged at the thick-thewed chieftain and swung him around. For an instant they were face to face, and Jim saw the rage in the grim old face, the fire in the furious eyes, the trail of spittle running down the bearded chin.

The chief clawed at Jim, then came charging forward, head lowered to butt. Jim rose high, locked his arm around the thick neck, levered downward and then upward in a quick, instinctive hold.

The chief went flying high over the runners of the sled and came down on the ice with a solid thud, landing on his back. He lay there a moment as if stunned. The sled sped onward, and by the time the Dooney leader was on his feet, a hundred yards separated him from his humiliators.

Panting, Jim glanced at his father. "You all right, Dad?"

"No damage. Just shaken up. I never thought your judo would be so useful," Dr. Barnes said.

91

Jim glanced back. The tribesmen were still running, scattering in every direction. Alone and storming, the old chief was doing a dance of tempestuous rage on the ice, leaping up and down and ripping at his clothes.

From the other sled, Ted Callison called, "We've got to stop! We need Carl!"

"Someone hurt?" Dr. Barnes yelled back.

"It's Dom! The chief's spear got him—"

Jim caught his breath. Things had happened so quickly as they burst from the ring of spears that he had forgotten all about that wild spear-cast toward the other sled. He stood up suddenly, looked across to Ted's sled, twenty feet away.

Dom Hannon lay slumped in the back, against a folded tent. His parka was stained with red, and the shaft of the chief's spear projected from the lower part of his chest.

The sleds ground to a halt in a shower of ice chips. The Dooney folk were too far in the distance to matter now. Jim and Carl ran to the other sled, with Dave and Dr. Barnes not far behind.

Jim had never seen anyone look so pale. Dom was like a waxen image of himself. He lay limp and unconscious, arms and legs dangling bonelessly. His face was deathly white, and he looked old and shrunken, his whole body seeming even smaller and more wiry than it actually was.

Dr. Barnes opened Dom's parka while Carl readied the medic kit. Carl looked pale himself —he was, after all, only a policeman with first-aid training, not a surgeon.

The layers of clothing were drawn back. Jim bit his lip in sudden dismay as he saw how deeply the spear had penetrated. It was no scratch. The entire bone tip had slashed through clothing and flesh, had buried itself six inches in Dom's body. The angry old barbarian had cast his spear with a mighty thrust.

Carl looked up doubtfully. "We've got to get that spear out of him," he said, "But the point is barbed—"

"Cut it out," Dr. Barnes said. "Cut away the shaft first, and then try to slice through the barbs."

Jim forced himself to watch. Carl worked delicately, but blood spurted all the same. Away came the shaft of the spear, and then, using bone snippers, Carl sheared through the barbs of the point and wiggled it free of the wound. Blood gushed, a river of it. How much blood did someone as thin as Dom have, anyway? How much could he afford to lose?

"Hand me the sterilizer," Carl said softly.

Jim peered down, shaken by the sight of the wound. It seemed to him that Dom's whole chest had been laid open. Was that his heart, throbbing in there? What were those coiling, thrashing serpents in his body?

After a long moment Jim moved away, and climbed out of the sled. He peered to the westward, saw the tiny dots of the Dooney folk far to their rear. Then, shrugging heavily, he scuffed at the loose layer of snow above the ice, and went back to the other sled to wait.

It seemed as though days went by. But the sun was still high in the heavens when Carl and Dr. Barnes rose, long-faced and dark of visage. Carl's hands were covered with blood, and smears of blood stained his light blond hair. Jim looked across, and saw his father slowly shaking his head.

"It's no use," Dr. Barnes said. "Only a miracle could have saved him. We just aren't miracle workers."

They hewed a grave in the ice, and laid Dom to rest six feet down, and covered the place over, leaving no marker, for who could tell what desecration would be performed on him if they marked where he lay?

When the job was done, they entered the sleds and journeyed sadly onward.

The Dooney folk had had their toll after all.

_____ **8**

# *A Sea of Ice*

THE FOLLOWING MORNING THE SLOPE LEVELED OUT, and they knew they had reached the Atlantic. There was no rejoicing. The day was another cold, bleak one, and their mood of mourning deepened. Behind them now lay the entire American continent—and the body of one of their number.

The nature of their journey was changing at this point. Thus far they had traveled over mile-thick glacier with solid land beneath. But the glacier had thinned in a gentle slope of more than a hundred miles, sweeping down to the edge of the sea. Now the sea lay before them—a sea of ice,

95

frozen solid as far as the eye could tell, but treacherous of underpinning, unpredictable, dangerous. From here until they reached the European continent, the menace of an ice breakup would hover over them. They would never know whether the ice beneath the runners of their sled was sixty feet thick, or six hundred, or six inches—until the moment when they crashed through the fragile crust.

It *looked* solid enough. That was all they could go by.

Dr. Barnes decided on a cautious approach, at least at the outset. Halting the sleds, he explained that someone would have to walk out onto the ice and test its strength. "If it'll bear one man's weight, of course, that's still no guarantee it'll hold up under a sled. But at least this way we'll know if it's really weak."

They drew lots, and Chet Farrington was chosen. He seemed unperturbed. "Just be ready to fish me out fast if I go under," he told them.

He started out on the ice.

He walked the first twenty feet as though he were walking on a bridge of glass, spanning a mile-deep abyss. Taking step after gingerly step, he edged out onto the shining white surface of the ice pack. But he seemed to build up confidence as he went along. Soon he was striding merrily, jauntily. He was a quarter of a mile away when he turned and waved to the men in the sleds.

Another twenty yards and he was dancing on the ice, jumping up and down to test its strength. Again and again he bounded up, landed with both boots digging into the ice, and strode on. In ten minutes he was only a dot in the distance.

"Looks safe enough," Ted Callison said. "At least this part. I'm for going."

Dr. Barnes nodded. "So am I," he said. "But one sled at a time. There's no sense doubling the risk."

"Okay," Ted said. "My sled goes, then. You follow us if we don't get into any trouble."

The sled slid forward. It carried only two passengers, Ted and Roy Veeder.

Jim watched, taut-nerved, ready to scramble out onto the ice if the sled broke through and slipped into water. But nothing went wrong. Picking up speed as it went, the sled edged out steadily onto the ice pack, and soon it had caught up to Chet, far in the distance.

Jim looked at his father. He nodded. Dave Ellis, at the controls of their sled, opened the throttle and they set out after Ted and Roy and Chet. Soon, both sleds were side by side, moving speedily and smoothly over the ice.

It swiftly became evident that their extra caution had been unnecessary—at least this close to shore. The ice felt solid and substantial beneath them. Probably the pack was several hundred feet thick here, sturdy enough to support any number of sleds.

They halted in midafternoon. Ted's sled was far in the lead at that point, but it came to a stop and waited for the other to catch up with it.

What looked like open water lay just ahead.

"It's a lake," Ted told them. "I scouted it while I was waiting for you. We'll have to detour. It's at least a mile long, but there's solid ice all around it."

"Just a big hole in the ice," Roy Veeder added. "I wonder what it's doing here?"

97

They parked the sleds and advanced on foot to inspect the open water. Oddly, the ice seemed sturdy right up to the edge of the "lake." It was as though some giant had spooned out a great chunk of ice, and had filled the gaping hole with water.

"Summer melt is beginning," Dave Ellis remarked. "There must be a warm current passing through here that keeps this little stretch clear." He knelt at the edge, broke off a brittle chunk of waterlogged ice. "See? It's starting to melt back. This hole will probably double in size by July, and then gradually freeze again through the winter."

"Does it go right down to the bottom?" Carl asked.

Dave grinned. "Your guess is as good as mine. But it looks to be at least a hundred feet deep. Maybe it goes clear down to the sea itself."

Jim walked out on the rim of the crater in the ice field, and looked down. The water was so blue it seemed almost black. He cupped the palm of his hand, drew a little water up, tasted it.

"Salty," he said. "I think it's ocean water."

"I've got an idea," Chet Farrington announced suddenly. "I'm going to go fishing!"

Everyone laughed—everyone but Chet, who turned out to be dead serious. As a zoologist, he said, he wanted to get a close-up look at fish, after having studied them secondhand all his life. "Besides," he admitted, "they say that fish are good to eat."

"Are you a zoologist or just somebody who's always hungry?" Roy Veeder wanted to know.

"Both," Chet said blandly. He ran back to the sleds and rummaged in the supply stores until he found a thirty-foot length of wire. He bent one end of it into a sharp hook and embedded a synthetic food pellet on it. To the general amusement of all, he sat down by the edge of the water and cast the line in, and waited as though he expected to be pulling fish out by the dozen at any moment.

Jim and some of the others stood by him. All animal life was new and full of wonder for Jim as much as for Chet, and he longed to see a fish, to touch its scaly sides, to examine its gills. But when ten minutes had passed without a nibble on Chet's line, Jim started to give up hope.

Back at the sled, Ted Callison had the radio set out again. His face was set in an expression of rigid concentration as he delicately adjusted the dials.

There was the crackle of static, the sputter of noise . . .

And then a voice.

"London, yes. Who is this, please?"

"New York calling. Callison, Ted Callison. I'm with Raymond Barnes and his party. Is this Noel Hunt?"

"Can't hear you, New York!"

"Is—this—Noel—Hunt—?"

"Go on, New York," came the reply. "We are getting you now, New York."

Ted pinwheeled his arm to signal the others. Jim ran to his father, who was studying the ice near the edge of the water, and called, "Ted's got London on the radio, Dad!"

They gathered around—all but Chet, who went on dangling his line stolidly as though the entire success of their journey depended on his luck as a fisherman.

Jim heard the tinny words: "You've left New York, you say?"

"That's right," Ted said eagerly. "Eight of us—no, seven, now. We're on our way across the ice. We're coming to visit London!"

"Is this an official party?"

Callison looked to Dr. Barnes for advice. The tall man shook his head slightly.

"No," Ted said. "Not official. Just—just seven people coming to London. We've already gone about a hundred fifty miles. We should reach you within a month."

"How are you traveling?"

"By sled," Ted said. "We're coming across the ice."

"But how will you cross the water?"

"What water?"

"The Atlantic!"

"So far it's frozen," Ted replied. "Mostly, anyway. We hope to make it all the way across. We'll be seeing you soon, London!"

"Why—why are you coming?" the faint voice out of the speaker said, perplexed.

"Why?" Ted asked. "Why not? It's time for a visit, isn't it? Three hundred years underground is long enough. We're on our way, London!"

There was silence from the other end, strange after Ted's jubilant whoop. Jim frowned. Why no word of encouragement, why no expression of excitement? The Londoner seemed merely baffled that anybody should want to undertake so arduous and improbable a journey.

"Are you still there, London?" Ted asked after a moment.

"Yes. Yes. But—all right, New York. Good-by, now. Good-by, New York!"

"Hello?" Ted said. "Hello, hello, hello!"

100

He looked up, shaking his head, and turned off the set.

"They don't sound very friendly, do they?" Jim said.

"Maybe he was just startled," Carl suggested. "After all, to find out that an expedition is actually coming across the Atlantic—"

Dr. Barnes shook his head. "Even so, he might have seemed a little more enthusiastic. I wonder what sort of welcome we're in for, when we reach the other side. If we make it."

They were ready to leave. All but Chet. He had not eaten lunch with them, he had not helped to charge the sleds; he still sat by the edge of the water, long legs folded weirdly underneath him, patiently dangling his line into the water.

"Should we leave him behind?" Ted Callison asked. "He doesn't need us, anyway. He can live off the fish he catches."

"Then he'll go hungry," Roy said. "He hasn't caught one yet, has he?"

Chet ignored the banter. He peered into the dark water as though trying to hocus fish onto his line with sheer will power. Suddenly he stiffened and tugged at the line.

"I've got a bite!" he yelled. "Something took the bait!"

"Reel it in, man!" Ted Callison urged him. "Maybe you've caught a whale!"

The shining line came up out of the water. Chet stared in dismay. A wriggling, flopping creature no more than five inches long dangled from the end of his line.

"Some whale!" Ted Callison roared.

101

"A monster!" Carl whooped.

Chet's embarrassment seemed to overwhelm his scientific curiosity. Red-faced, he muttered a curse and made as if to throw the tiny fish back into the water without even pausing to examine it.

"Wait," Jim said. "Let me see!"

He took the line and held it up. The fish was beautiful. Its sleek, scaly body glimmered like quicksilver in the sunlight. Beady eyes looked at him in mute appeal. The little creature's body seemed perfectly designed, shaped by a master hand, magnificently streamlined for a life in the water. Fascinated, Jim studied it a long moment. Then, carefully, he disengaged the hook and returned the fish to the water. It sped away like a streak of flame and was lost to sight.

Jim remained, staring at the water.

"What's the matter?" Ted asked him. "You hypnotized or something?"

"It was a fish," Jim said. "I saw a fish!"

"Of course you did. What of it?"

"How many fish did you ever see in New York?"

"Why, none," Ted said. "So?"

Jim shook his head. "You don't understand, do you? Doesn't it excite you to be up here, seeing something new every day? Animals, fish—the sun, the moon, the stars—"

"Well, sure, those things are interesting," Ted agreed.

"It's more than just *interesting* to see them," Jim insisted. He fumbled for words. "It's—it's—oh, I don't know, it's like discovering the whole world all at once. It makes me feel dizzy. I want to grab hold of the moon and the sky. I want to sing loud enough to be heard down in New York. Just seeing a little squirming fish makes me feel that way. Do you realize we're the first New Yorkers to see a fish since—since around the year twenty-three hundred?"

Jim realized that Ted was looking at him as if he had gone insane.

"You *don't* understand, do you?" Jim asked quietly.

The short, stocky man shrugged. "You're just overenthusiastic about being up here," he said. "I guess it's a natural reaction, when you're young. You'll outgrow it."

"I hope I don't," Jim shot back at him. "I wouldn't want to get as crusty and cantankerous as you are—Methuselah."

He sensed that Ted was having some fun with him. Callison was only twenty-four, after all, which didn't really give him the right to regard himself as a patriarch and Jim as a child.

Ted grinned suddenly and threw his arm around Jim's shoulders. "Sure," he said. "I think it's the greatest thing in the world to be looking a fish in the eye. I mean that. Otherwise why would I be here?"

Later that day they had an entirely different kind of creature look them in the eye.

They were on their way around the lake, which was turning out to be bigger than Ted's first estimate had it. Having traveled three miles to the north, they were beginning to curve eastward again. They were sledding over solid ice a hundred fifty yards from the edge of the water when the creature bobbed up out of the depths and regarded them curiously.

It was enormous. It stood shoulder-high out of the water, and a huge head decked with two fierce-looking tusks confronted them. Flippers sprouted where arms should have been. The creature looked like some grotesque parody of mankind, with its whiskers and its solemn little eyes, but no human being had ever had two-foot-long tusks like those.

"What is it?" Jim asked in a hushed voice.

"Walrus, I think," Chet Farrington said. "Relative of the seals, if that helps you any. Mammal. Lives in cold water."

Jim fingered the stud of his power torch. "Do you think he's going to attack?"

"Best I remember from my natural history books, they aren't flesh-eaters," Chet said. "They live off shellfish."

"He doesn't *look* unfriendly," said Roy Veeder.

Indeed, he seemed positively friendly. He was at the edge of the ice, now, flippers leaning out onto the ice shelf, and he was regarding them quizzically and with great curiosity, showing no sign of fear. The vast beast looked gentle and intelligent.

"Wait a second," Chet said. "I want a closer look."

"Same here," said Jim.

They left the sled and walked slowly toward the walrus. At close range it looked even stranger, Jim thought. But when he had come within a hundred feet of it, it turned and slipped into the water, and vanished from sight with astonishing speed.

Later that afternoon they encountered the walrus again, or one of his relatives. But this time the meeting was a less peaceful one. The walrus was under attack!

104

A group of fur-clad hunters had somehow lured the creature up onto the ice and had cut off its retreat to the water. Surrounding it, they were stabbing at it with wicked-looking spears of bone. When the sleds came upon the scene, the New Yorkers quickly detoured and headed away. One encounter with spear-wielding huntsmen had been enough for a while. The hunters were too busy with the walrus to pay attention to the party of travelers that had come upon them. Jim looked back, awed by the bulk of the beleaguered creature that reared nearly a dozen feet into the air, snorting and howling at its attackers, and then flopped helplessly down on the ice again as the hunters closed in for the kill. Jim felt a pang of sadness as he watched the nightmare scene of death being enacted on the ice. The walrus had seemed so gentle, so friendly. And now here he was, bleeding from a dozen wounds, succumbing to the onslaught of men.

Jim forced himself to be realistic. Men must eat. There were no hydroponics laboratories on the ice pack, no factories for the manufacture of synthetic foods. The walrus was food—thousands of pounds of it. His tusks, his bones, would all be useful as knives and utensils; his thick hide would go for clothing, his fat for oil, his very sinews for rope and for cord. Every day was a struggle for life, in the ice-world, and where man and walrus shared the same habitat, only one outcome was possible.

The struggle seemed over now. The walrus lay still.

Two of the hunters detached themselves from the group and began to run after the sleds, shouting.

"They see us," Jim said. "What do they want?"

"They're waving to us," Dave Ellis said. "They want us to stop. Here we go again!"

"Halt the sled," Dr. Barnes ordered. "Let's see what they want."

Dave looked startled. "But—"

"They aren't armed. Halt the sled!"

Dave eased the sled to a halt. Nearby, Ted Callison had brought the other sled to a stop also. The two huntsmen, panting and gasping, came running up alongside.

"Strangers!" they called. "Wait, strangers! Wait!"

They spoke English. Simply from their appearance, they seemed as far beyond the unfriendly Dooney folk of the shore as the Dooneys had been beyond the primitive, monosyllabic hunters that had been encountered farther inland. These two were tall and straight-backed and clean-shaven, and seemed almost like New Yorkers dressed in fur garments, rather than savages of fierce and bestial ways.

One of them, a lanky, blue-eyed man of about thirty, his lean face tanned and wind-toughened, called out to them, "Why do you flee? Claim your guest-rights!"

"We do not understand," Dr. Barnes replied.

"There has been a kill," the blue-eyed hunter answered, pointing to the fallen walrus. "You are strangers come among us. The law of hospitality requires us to feed you. Why flee, then?"

Dr. Barnes frowned. "We come from far off," he said slowly. "We do not know your ways. The last people we met had no law of hospitality. They attacked us and took a life."

"Who were they? What was their tribe-name?"

"They called themselves the Dooney folk."

"*Pah!* Inlanders! Savages!" the blue-eyed man exclaimed, while his silent companion shook his fist angrily in the general direction of the shore. "You can expect no better from them. But we are different. Come. You are our guests."

_____ **9**

# *"It Cannot Be Done!"*

IT WAS UNTHINKABLE TO REFUSE. THE BLUE-EYED MAN, who gave his name as Kennart and said he was son of the chief of the Jersey people, was obviously not expecting no for an answer. Dr. Barnes signaled to Ted, and both sleds reversed and headed back toward the hunters.

It was a pleasant novelty not to have to defend themselves against these people of the ice-world. It was even more agreeable to be treated as guests, even if they had little choice about accepting Jersey hospitality.

They returned to the site of the walrus kill, where two dozen Jersey hunters were slashing up the bulky corpse even more skillfully than the inlanders had sliced up their kill of moose. The Jerseys stared in surprise and fascination at the sleds, but there was no trace of fear or suspicion about them. Most of them, Jim noticed, were of the same blond-haired, blue-eyed type as Kennart himself. For an outsider, it was difficult to tell one from another, and Jim decided they were probably all descended from a small, closely related group.

Since Carl, too, was blond-haired and blue-eyed, he was the object of considerable interest. Kennart pointed to him and said, "Have you Jersey blood?"

"I doubt it," Carl said in confusion. "That is —well, I'm not sure."

Kennart laughed. "You look like one of us! Of what tribe are you, then?"

"Well—I'm from New York," Carl stammered. "The—the policeman tribe."

Kennart shook his head. "I know not these Pleecemans. Come you from the north?"

"No," Carl said. He looked to Jim for help.

Jim said, "We come from the west. From up there."

Kennart's eyes flashed. His hand darted out, caught Jim's wrist in an iron grip. "*Inlanders*? You say you are inlanders? That cannot be! Inlanders are animals! They speak another language, they live like beasts! Speak truth when you are my guest, stranger. From where come you?"

Jim did not flinch as the bone-crushing grip tightened. He said in a level voice, "We come from the west, but we are not inlanders. We come out of the Earth itself. We come from New York, a city beneath the ice."

He could not have staggered Kennart more

thoroughly if he had rammed him in the gut with his boot. The Jersey leader let go of Jim's arm, took a few faltering steps backward, turned pale beneath his deep tan. His jaw sagged, and for a moment he was speechless.

"No," he muttered finally. "It cannot be! From under the ice—? You make sport of me, no?"

"I speak only the truth," Jim told him. "We came up out of the ice, four, five days ago. We travel eastward."

"It is only a legend!" Kennart cried. "There are not really cities under the ice!" Then he bit his lip, and began to tremble. "Forgive me," he said to Jim in a hoarse whisper. "It is not right to give guests the lie." He came close, and one calloused hand reached up to touch Jim's cheek. "Your skin," Kennart muttered. "Soft. Not like our skin. Your strange clothing—your speech—everything about you—like nothing I have known before." He moistened his lips. "It is really true? You have come up out of the ice?"

"It is really true," Jim said.

They reached the Jersey encampment an hour later, and when the sun had nearly dipped into the western ice field and the sky was rapidly darkening. The fair-haired hunters were camped on the far side of the lake. Thirty or more igloos sprouted like mushrooms from the ice, and nearly the entire tribe, more than a hundred strong, turned out to greet the strange new guests. The Jersey women, like their men, were light of complexion, though all were deeply tanned wherever bare skin showed. In the case of the very small children, a great deal of skin showed; despite the bitter twenty-five-degree cold, some youngsters no more than five or six years old wore nothing but a strip of fur around their waists, and loose sandals of hide.

These were a very sturdy folk, Jim realized, shivering in his warm garments. But they had had generations to adapt to the brutal conditions of the ice-world. They knew nothing warmer.

None of the Jerseys seemed at all elderly—none of the men gathered round the sleds appeared to be as old as forty, nor were any of the women middle-aged. Jim wondered about that. Were the old ones still in the igloos? Or were there simply no old ones? Life might be short here in the ice-world, Jim realized darkly. Once a man had ceased to serve his function as a hunter, he would only be a burden on the tribe. Jim suspected that among the Jerseys the aged did not meet a natural death, and he shuddered a little at the thought.

The seven men from the sleds entered the circle of igloos. Women and children crowded round, now and then boldly coming forward to touch the arm or the shoulder of one of the strangers. Jim heard them whispering, and caught snatches of sentences. "City under the ice," he heard. "How pale they look!" "They come from the west!"

Kennart led them toward the centermost igloo. "You must meet my father," he declared. "Then there will be a feast in your honor. Wait here a moment."

They waited outside what was obviously the chief's dwelling, while Kennart entered to bear the news to the head of the tribe. He emerged, minutes later, and gestured for them to enter.

The igloo's entrance was low, and Jim ducked going in. He was surprised to find, once he was

inside, that the roof was comfortably high, allow-
ing him to stand erect. One after another, his
comrades followed him in.

By the dim light of flickering oil lamps, Jim
made out three figures sitting against the far side
of the igloo. Here, then, were the old ones of the
tribe, or at least a few of them. They looked as
ancient as Mayor Hawkes, looked like men ninety
years old or more. Yet one of them was Kennart's
father, and Kennart could be no more than thirty.
Men aged rapidly in this harsh world, Jim thought.

"You are welcome among us," the most
commanding-looking of the three ancients said in
a dry, cracking voice. Although he sat wrapped in
furs like an invalid, he was regal and imposing in
presence for all his appearance of age, and from
the breadth of his shoulders Jim guessed that the
chief had been a giant among men, perhaps close
to seven feet in height. "I am Lorin of the Jerseys,"
the chief went on. "My son tells me you are of the
New Yorks. I know not this tribe."

One of the old men at Lorin's side whispered
something to him in a brittle, rasping voice. The
chief frowned, ran a shaky hand through the still
flourishing mane of white hair that topped his
head, and peered at the strangers in curiosity.

The chief said, "You have told my son you come
up from out of the ice. Garold here says New York
is the name of a lost city of the Great Ones. Are
these things true?"

Dr. Barnes stepped forward. "They are true," he
said. "We come from New York, which lies under
the great ice mountain to the west. We journey
eastward toward another city in the ice called
London."

"How many are you, of this New York tribe?"

Dr. Barnes hesitated. "Eight hundred thousand," he said finally.

Lorin looked blank. In a whisper that was clearly audible, he asked his two venerable advisers, "What number is that?"

Garold, to his left, shrugged and looked confused. But the other old man, mumbling to himself for a moment, turned finally to the chief and said, "It is eighty hundred hundreds, sire."

"Eighty hundred hundreds," Lorin repeated slowly. "Eighty hundred hundreds?" Suddenly a look of wrath came into his eyes, and he seemed to be struggling to get to his feet, only to fall back as weak legs failed to support him. "Kennart!" he roared, in a voice charged with fury. "Have you brought them to mock me? Eighty hundred hundreds in their tribe! I am no fool, Kennart!"

Kennart said softly, "I have reason to believe they speak truth, father."

"Eighty hundred hundreds!" Lorin muttered. "It cannot be! There are not eighty hundred hundreds in the entire world, and they say they have so many in their tribe alone!"

"Our city is great," Dr. Barnes said. "It is built in passageways many miles long, one above the other. I speak the truth when I tell you how many folk there are there. Once there were many more people than that in New York—before the ice came. Once eighty *hundred* hundred of hundreds lived in New York, and even more. But that was long ago."

Lorin conferred with his two sages again. Finally, looking up, apparently satisfied, he said, "You will be our guests, then. You will tell us about your

113

city of eighty hundred hundreds. You will share our food. Kennart! Ready the feast!''

Jim had feared another meal of raw meat. But his apprehensions were needless. The Jerseys cooked their food.

The whole tribe assembled out of doors, though by now night had fallen and the temperature was rapidly dropping toward the zero mark. Blankets of hide were spread on the ice, round a blazing oil fire.

Jim saw that the only aged members of the tribe were the three in Lorin's igloo, the chief and his two advisers. They were crippled, bowed down with age and disease, and younger men helped them to their place by the fire. Evidently one had to be very wise to survive to a ripe old age in this tribe! There was no room for those who could not contribute strength or wits to the needs of the Jerseys.

The seven guests were favored with a place of honor—near the fire, next to the chief himself. Kennart sat with them. Boys of the tribe served them, so that they did not have to rise to get their food.

The feast commenced with a dark drink, served in cups fashioned from the skulls of small animals. It was a grisly touch, Jim thought, wondering what small creatures of the ice packs had given their lives so that men might drink. Yet he had to admire the ingenuity of the Jerseys, of all these ice-worlders. Without metal, without stone, without wood, without clay for pottery, without building materials of any sort, they had somehow managed to make do with bone and hide alone, meeting all their domestic needs.

Just what it was they were drinking, Jim never knew. It was dark red, and oily, and cold, and the taste was sweet and faintly sickening. He hesitated only a moment, and then, seeing his father drain his cup, put his own to his lips. It was only fitting. The Jerseys were making a great sacrifice, sharing their hard-won food with these strangers. A guest must be a guest, then, and welcome gladly whatever was offered.

The second course was fish, served on flat plates of leather. Each of them got a foot-long fish, head, tail, scales and all. They were given no utensils but a bone knife.

Ted Callison nudged Jim in the ribs. "You wanted to see what a fish looks like? Here's your chance!"

Jim grinned sourly. He picked up his fish, wondering how to attack it. He glanced at Kennart, who was busily slitting the fish down the back, splitting it in half the thin way, and peeling the fragile bones out of the meat. Seeing that he was being watched, Kennart grinned heartily, and demonstrated for Jim by picking up the fish and taking a healthy bite. Jim went to work with the knife, clumsily slicing the fish in imitation of what Kennart had done.

Kennart said, "How eat you fish in New York?"

"We have no fish there," Jim said. "No fish, no animals of any kind."

Kennart looked shocked. "What do you eat, then?"

"Hydroponically raised vegetables and synthetic

115

protein," Jim said. "Algae steak and—" He paused. "None of that makes any sense to you, does it?"

"They are strange words," Kennart admitted. "Hydro—vege—synthe—I know not those words. They are city words. New York words. Your world must be a strange one."

"Not to us," Jim said.

"No. Not to you."

Jim managed to eat the fish without serious difficulty, not even swallowing any of the tiny bones. Almost before he had finished, along came the next course—roasted meat of some sort. A leather platter was placed before each of them. Jim eyed its contents doubtfully, but did not hesitate to dig in.

"You eat the heart of the walrus now," Kennart told them. "It is your right, as guests, to have the courage-part."

Jim gulped, but went on eating. They had filled his cup again, he noticed, and he took a deep drink to wash down the meat. It struck him that what he was drinking was very likely blood, mixed perhaps with melted ice. Doggedly he ate on. A guest must be a guest, he reminded himself.

The feast seemed endless. There was more roast meat, and then what seemed to be chunks of pure fat, and after that a course of dried meat with a pungent, tangy flavor and a consistency approximately that of chunks of iron. Round and round went the serving-boys, offering food with a generosity that was almost terrifying. Dr. Barnes set an example for the others, devouring the food with a voracity Jim had never seen in his father before. Jim wondered whether it was really right to eat so much of the Jerseys' food, but the more the visitors ate, the more delighted the Jerseys seemed to be.

At last the meal was over. At last!

Jim felt stuffed to the bursting point. He was laden with strange foods, swollen and bloated, and he felt that a sudden poke in the ribs might have disastrous consequences. He was flushed from overeating, so that he scarcely noticed the sharp cold, hardly minded the cutting wind that swept across the ice plain from the east. It was dark now. The full moon had sped its course, and tonight only a bright sliver, the last quarter, remained. Jim was baffled by that. The night before, Dave Ellis had tried to explain something to him of the phases of the moon, but it had all been too abstract, too theoretical for easy understanding. One who has lived all his life in a cavern beneath the surface of the earth does not readily grasp the subtleties of astronomy.

When the remains of the meal had been cleared away, the whole tribe fell silent. It was time for after-dinner speeches, Jim thought, and he was right.

Lorin, the chief, lifted one hand. Without rising, he declared. "We are with guests tonight. From the west they come, from New York, a city under the ice. Eighty hundreds of hundreds live in their city." A murmur of disbelief swept through the tribesmen. Lorin glared at them. *"Eighty hundreds of hundreds!"* he repeated vehemently. "Of them, seven come tonight. We bid them welcome among us for as long as they care to stay."

Lorin signaled, and two young Jerseys rose and came forward, burdened with things wrapped in a hide.

117

The chief said, "We offer gifts to show friendship, men of New York."

The hides were unwrapped, and one gift after another was laid at the feet of Dr. Barnes, the "chief" of the visitors. Two long spears of bone, elegantly carved with incised abstract patterns; a superb bone knife; a robe of fur; fine sandals over whose stitching some Jersey woman had labored long and hard. When the gifts had been bestowed, Dr. Barnes nodded solemnly toward the chief, then toward his advisers, toward Kennart, and finally toward all the tribe.

"I offer my thanks," he said humbly. "We will treasure these magnificent gifts as memories of our stay with the Jersey folk. We can offer little in return, since we are but wanderers, but we beg you take our poor offering."

Dr. Barnes gestured, and it was Jim's turn to rise. Dr. Barnes had shrewdly guessed that the feast would include an exchange of gifts, and the New Yorkers had come prepared.

Jim advanced and stood before the chief to present the gifts. One by one he laid down an ice hatchet of tempered steel, a keen metal hunting knife, one of the extra parkas, a burned-out power tube from the sled, and several other small things which could be of no conceivable use to the Jerseys except as trophies to display and ponder, but which made fine gifts all the same.

Lorin examined each gift with evident delight. He nodded finally. "It is well. You are truly generous, men of New York, and your kind is welcome among us forever."

The gifts were carefully bundled up and placed to one side. Then attention turned to one of the chief's advisers, the venerable and withered Garold, who launched into a chant that was obviously a formal part of every tribal feast.

It was hard for the visitors to understand what he was saying, partly because of the difference in the pronunciation of the Jersey people, partly because Garold's voice was weak and quavery with age, and partly because of the singsong intonation he used. For the first few moments, Jim thought Garold was speaking in some language other than English. Then he caught a phrase or two that he could understand, and, fascinated, strained to hear.

What Garold was reciting was an epic poem of historical events—an *Iliad* of the Ice Age. In a world without writing, Jim realized, this was the only way history could be transmitted from generation to generation—through the oral tradition, an old man chanting by the fireside after the tribal feast. The Jerseys seemed to know Garold's poem well, for as he went along, Jim heard them quietly murmuring the words to themselves, though Garold spoke rapidly, slurring over his syllables as though the recital were a mere ritual, a conveying of things long familiar to everyone.

He began, apparently, by talking of the world before the ice came—the great cities with their "hundred hundreds" of people. He mentioned names, distorted and altered through the retellings, Nyok and Chago, Filelfa, Bosin. "The land was green with trees," he chanted, "and grass covered the plains, and on the highway was the car, in the air flew the airplane."

"*In the air flew the airplane,*" muttered the tribesmen like a responding congregation.

119

What could they know, Jim wondered, of trees and grass, of highways and cars, of airplanes? These things were only hazy blurs to *him*, and he had studied history in school, had seen photos of the world as it once had been. To these people, the words they mumbled could have no possible meaning. Why, even the color *green* must be a mystery to them, in this land of white and blue and black!

"Then came the ice," Garold was chanting. "Covering all, covering field and covering city, covering the world." He sang of how people fled, how some dug holes in the ground in which to hide, how others headed southward, how the world's life died as the advancing snow and ice devoured everything.

Then, Garold said, the snow stopped falling. The Gods relented, and the worst was past. First to return to the old lands were the Sea People, the Jerseys and the Ninglanders and the Carolinas. These, Jim guessed, were small tribes who lived on the frozen ocean, where food was relatively abundant, fish and walrus to be caught in the places where the water was open.

And then other survivors of the great freeze returned to live on top of the glaciers. This part of the story was hard to follow, almost incoherent, but there was no mistaking the contempt in the old man's voice for the "inlanders." He seemed to distinguish between those tribes that lived along the slope, the eastern edge of what had been North America, and those who lived high on the glacier itself. The slope people—the Dooneys and others like them—were rough and uncouth, and could not be trusted, but at least they still spoke what Garold called "The language of men," and understood civilized ways even though they did not abide by them. The real inlanders, though, were nothing but wild men, savages who spoke in animal-like grunts, beast-men who had cast off every trace of the old civilization.

The farther from the sea, the more difficult were the living conditions. Inland, food was scarce, and civilization itself crumbled under the need simply to stay alive. The Sea People had maintained an elaborate civilization, with ceremony and history and a language not very much changed over the years. The people of the slope, living in a somewhat harsher environment, had slipped backward toward savagery, but not as far as the inlanders whose every effort had to go toward mere survival.

It was probably accurate, Jim thought, comparing the hostile Dooneys to the first tribe of nomads they had met, the moose hunters. The primitive inlanders, though they had been hostile at first, had easily been awed by Carl's display of medical skill, and had ended by kneeling in homage to him. The semicivilized Dooneys, just as unfriendly at first, had also been awed, by the display of the power torch's destructive ability, but they had claimed a life, all the same, and they knew enough English to demand a toll of strangers. Of the two, Jim thought, he preferred the simpler folk, though he was hardly delighted by the way they had been ready to leave their injured comrade to die.

Garold went on. The epic turned to the future now, and became prophetic. The sun would shine, he said, and the ice would melt, and the world would turn warm. Life would become easy and gentle, and the Jerseys would dwell in a paradise on Earth.

"And the people of the cities will come up out of the ground," Garold said. "In their hundreds of hundreds they will arise, and bring wonders to us, and live with us in friendship."

The Jerseys looked a trifle surprised at those lines. Jim realized that Garold must have departed from the script here, adding a few passages of his own to the familiar story. Speaking more slowly, as if he were improvising, Garold told of how seven strangers had come out of the west, riding in wonderful sleighs, and how they had eaten at the fireside of the Jersey folk, and how they had described the wonders of their city of New York. The narration ended at that point, the old man sinking back tiredly while the tribe—and then the visitors, in imitation—hammered their hands palm down on the ice in applause.

Dr. Barnes turned to Jim and said quietly, "We're famous now. We probably will have a permanent place in their saga."

Jim grinned. "I'd love to hear it twenty years from now, after they've had some time to embellish it a little. They'll have the sleds flying through the air before they're through."

Then his expression clouded. "It's too bad Dom couldn't have been here to listen to that saga, though," Jim said quietly. "He'd have been fascinated by the language these people use."

The feast was clearly over, now. The Jerseys were getting up, heading back to their individual igloos, not without staring intently at the strangers

122

before they departed. Kennart said, "You will come to my father's dwelling before you sleep?"

The New Yorkers followed Kennart and Lorin into the chief's igloo. A fresh fire was lit, and then the chief fixed his keen eyes on Dr. Barnes and said, "Tell us, friends, of this city of London that you journey toward. Is it near?"

"No," Dr. Barnes said. "It lies on the other side of the sea. It is—it is thirty hundreds of miles from here."

Lorin frowned. "So far? You will go so far, across the sea? But do your sleighs travel over open water?"

"No," Dr. Barnes said.

"Then you cannot reach this city of London. It is impossible. It cannot be done!"

_____ **10**

## *Nothing Is Impossible*

THERE WAS A LONG MOMENT OF SILENCE IN THE IGLOO.
Then Dr. Barnes said slowly, "The great sea—it is
not frozen all the way across?"

"No," Lorin said. "There is open water. One
cannot see to the other side. One cannot get
across."

Jim's heart sank. This far, only to be stopped?

Dr. Barnes said, "Has anyone ever tried to cross?
A boat of ice, maybe—"

Kennart looked up. "There are those who cross
the sea," he said with a glance at his father. "They
cross in boats of wood."

"*Wood?*"

"They are seafarers. They fashion their boats in the southland, where it is warm, where wood can be had. They rove the open water to hunt the great fish. But they are not friendly. They are like the inlanders—savages."

"We could hire them," Dr. Barnes said. "Pay them to take us across."

"They will not do it," Lorin said flatly. "They will kill you. They kill all strangers."

"The Dooney folk didn't kill us," Dr. Barnes said. "The inlanders didn't kill us."

"The seafarers are savage men," Lorin insisted.

Dr. Barnes crossed his legs, gripped his knees tensely. "If we reached them, spoke to them, perhaps—"

The chief shook his head. "You will not even reach them," he declared. "You will die on the way. The ice is not strong. You will not know the way to travel, and you will fall into the sea and be lost."

The New Yorkers looked at each other in distress. Seafaring savages they could handle, perhaps, but this other menace—the weakness of the ice—was a far greater one.

"There are paths to the sea," Lorin went on. "We who live on the ice know those paths. But you —strangers, out of the Earth itself—how can you know them?"

Silence fell again. Then, unexpectedly, Kennart said, "I can show them the paths to the sea, father!"

Lorin looked startled. "*You?*"

"I will guide them over the ice to the place

125

where the seafarers come," Kennart said. "From then on they must fend for themselves, but I can help them at least so far."

Garold and the other old man tugged at the chief's robe, whispered urgently to him. Lorin nodded, closed his eyes a moment, then said, "You are the leader of our people, Kennart. You will be chief one day. If you die in the emptiness, what will become of us? I have no other sons."

A muscle flickered in Kennart's cheek. "These men are our guests, father," he said simply. "They have eaten our food and shared our fire."

"But—"

"There are other men who can be chief," Kennart declared. "Here are strangers who need help. Am I to hide here like a woman and let them go to their deaths?"

The argument told. Lorin bowed his head. The two wise men chattered and prodded him, but the chief brushed them off as though they were irritating insects. After a long pause Lorin looked at his guests, his pale blue eyes glittering by the light of the dim oil lamps.

He said, "It is done. I give you my son Kennart as a guide to the sea."

Dr. Barnes, looking drawn and strained, said, "I would not take the chief's son from the tribe. Perhaps another could go with us—"

"No!" Kennart whirled, his eyes blazing with anger. "I will go! It is my right! You are my guests! I brought you here, and I will take you away!"

Lorin nodded. "It is his right, city men. He will go with you, and you may not refuse. He will take you to the sea. After that you must go your own way."

They left in the morning, after a sound night's sleep. Kennart rode in the lead sled, along with Dr. Barnes, Jim, and Carl. Dave Ellis moved over to join Ted Callison, Chet, and Roy Veeder in the other sled.

Kennart had brought provisions with him: bundles of dried meat, of the sort that had been served at the banquet. It was not that he had any prejudice against the food the New Yorkers would serve him; he simply preferred his own.

Kennart seemed fascinated by the sled. He asked Jim to lift the engine hood, and he sat crouched in the rear of the sled for more than an hour, staring with gleaming eyes at the whirling turbines. But not once did he ask how the sled worked. He inspected it till he had had enough, and then he nodded and turned away, obviously so completely bewildered by it that he did not even care to begin asking questions.

It was a bright day, and they made good time. With Kennart guiding them, there was no slackening of the pace. By midmorning, when they halted for lunch, they were forty miles from the Jersey encampment. The broad ice field glinted in the sun; there seemed to be no end to it in any direction, nor did a sign of life break the bleakness of the scene anywhere, except for a few birds, now appearing this close to open water. Jim stared at the winged creatures in awe and delight.

Kennart ate silently, chewing on his dried meat with gusto. The toughness of the stuff gave him no trouble at all. Jim, after he had eaten, walked over to the fair-haired man, who promptly held forth some of his food.

Jim began to refuse. But it struck him that Kennart might be insulted, so he swallowed his words, smiled gratefully, and accepted a very small chunk of the meat. Eating the stony stuff was a chore.

Finally Jim said, "Tell me: how many days' journey is it to the open sea?"

Kennart pondered it. "As we have traveled this day? A seven days' journey or less."

"And as the Jerseys travel, how long would it take?"

Kennart shrugged. "Perhaps thirty days. Perhaps a little more."

"So much as that! We had no idea of that when we let you come with us."

"What does it matter to you?" Kennart asked.

Jim said, "Your tribe needs you. How will you get back, after you have brought us to the open water?"

"Let me worry about that."

"A thirty day trip—alone—over the ice—?"

"It will be no hardship," Kennart said. "I have food enough to last me. When I grow weary, there will be other tribes to make me a guest. Hospitality is sacred among us, friend Jim. I will not starve."

"Suppose you get lost? Suppose there's a storm?"

Kennart looked untroubled. Grinning, he said, "Among our people, when a boy passes fifteen years of age, he becomes a man. He must then take his manhood-journey. He goes off by himself for twelve moons and must not return to the tribe on pain of death. He must hunt and fish to stay alive,

128

and can speak to no other human being. If he returns safely, he is given a man's rights. It is an experience that leaves him ready to face any kind of danger in after life."

Jim shivered at the quiet phrase, "*If* he returns safely." The thought of boys of fifteen roaming the ice alone for a year left him shaken.

He said, "Are there many who—who don't return?"

"A few each year," Kennart said. "We forget their names as though they never existed." Getting to his feet, he stretched mightily and measured the height of the sun with a quick glance. "Are your sleighs ready to leave?" he asked. "We can make good distance yet today."

As they continued eastward, Jim considered Kennart's words. Small wonder that a month-long journey over the ice held no terrors for him if as a boy he had lasted a full year in the wasteland! Jim understood now why the Jerseys were so insistent upon giving hospitality; hospitality was a way of life here, where men might wander far from their tribes. And he understood, too, why the men of the Jersey tribe seemed so robust, so capable of withstanding any hardship. The weaklings, the unfit, were culled out in their teens. "We forget their names as though they never existed," Kennart had said. A cruel system? Perhaps—but necessary for a tribe that lived on the ice, where every bit of food counted, and where the weak would drag down the strong.

For three days they journeyed, and the trip became almost routine. The cold, the eye-dazzling glare of sun on ice, the nights of discomfort huddled on the floor of the tent—these things scarcely were noticed any longer. Kennart led them, traveling in wide zigzagging patterns to take them away from areas of thin ice. There were no landmarks out here, nor did Kennart use any kind of compass or other direction-finding instrument. How he operated was sheer mystery. He would stare at the ice field ahead, whisper to himself for a moment, then point off at a fifty-degree angle from their line of travel. They would change course, and later in the day some gap in the ice would become dimly visible in the distance along their old course. Did Kennart have some intuitive sense of danger, Jim wondered? Or were his senses sharper? Could he somehow *feel* a gathering weakness in the ice, and turn away from it? There was no fathoming his method.

On the fourth day from the Jersey encampment, Kennart announced suddenly, "From here it becomes very dangerous. The ice is unfriendly. We must go carefully."

There was no mistaking the tension in his eyes. They had come to a part of the frozen sea where even Kennart was worried, and that was cause for alarm. Up till now, Kennart's presence among them had lulled them into nearly forgetting that they were traveling across a crust of ice of uncertain thickness, beneath which lay water so cold that a man would die in it within minutes. For three days, they had had the illusion that all was solid beneath the runners of the sleds, as solid as the mile-thick glacier across which they had earlier come. Now, it was as though the ice might split and engulf them at any moment.

"Remain here," Kennart ordered them. "No one leave the sleds until I return."

He walked briskly away, and before long his broad-backed form was nothing but a speck against the ice. Ted Callison lifted his binoculars and peered after him.

"What's he doing?" Carl asked.

"Kneeling," Ted reported. "Praying. I think he's praying!"

Kennart remained alone on the ice for twenty minutes. When he returned, he looked taut-nerved, uncertain.

"The warm weather is coming," he told them. "The ice is strange this time of the year. I hear it groaning. It cries out for blood. Danger lies between us and the water. But we will go on. And we will reach the sea."

The sleds crept forward, speed held down to no more than a couple of miles an hour. Ominous cracking and splitting sounds seemed to rise from the ice, and now and then a far-off boom as of thunder. Kennart did not notice the sounds—or at least pretended not to notice them.

The sun was warm the following morning. Too warm, thought Jim, who found himself longing for zero-degree weather. In his mind's eye he saw droplets of water forming like beads on the underside of the ice pack, saw the ice growing thinner and thinner until it was only inches thick beneath them. After they had traveled for an hour, Kennart ordered the sleds to halt.

"From here to the sea," he said, "we must go on foot. The sleds can follow behind us. The ice is very unfriendly here."

131

Carl remained in one sled, Dave in the other, as drivers. Everyone else clambered out. Kennart shaped the group into a V-formation, with himself at the apex and the rest spread out behind him over the ice.

They walked and the sleds followed behind.

The ice field stretched ahead of them, clear to the horizon, so that it seemed to be an infinite trip to the sea. Still, the sun blazed in the east, leading them on. It was almost uncomfortably warm now, the temperature well up in the middle thirties, so that Jim found himself actually sweating inside his thick garments.

They plodded on.

The ice seemed solid enough beneath their feet, Kennart detoured several times that morning, detecting who knew what mysterious weakness in the underpinning, but to Jim it did not seem as though the ice was nearly as "unfriendly" as Kennart believed.

So when trouble struck, it was all the more tragic, coming as it did when they were just being lulled again into a sense of false confidence.

It happened with lightning swiftness, an hour after their halt for lunch. Kennart was well out in front. Jim and Chet flanked him, to the side and some thirty yards behind. In back of them came Dr. Barnes, Roy, and Ted, while Dave and Carl, in the sleds, brought up the rear. Jim had swung into a steady rhythm of march, *left*-right, *left*-right, *left*-right, and a kind of hypnosis gripped him, a dreamy mood of inattention brought on by the flat terrain and the whiteness of everything and the brightness of the sun and the monotony of the march.

He heard a sound as of breaking wood, and then a splash.

But what he had heard did not register on his mind for a long moment. Then he reacted slowly, like one coming up out of a drugged sleep.

To his left a sudden fissure yawned in the ice. For an instant, he saw dark water, gleaming in the sun, saw a hand wave briefly—and then nothing.

"Chet!" he yelled, and started to spring toward the place where the ice had opened.

"No!" Kennart cried, in an ear-splitting voice that could have been heard a continent away. "No, Jim! Stay back!"

Jim halted momentarily. Looking around, he saw Kennart sprinting toward him over the ice.

"It's Chet," Jim called. "He fell in!"

He started toward the place where Chet had been. Already, he saw in horror, the ice crack was closing again. A bare six-inch-wide line of darkness revealed the site of the crack now.

Jim had gone no more than three steps when Kennart caught up with him. The blond man's hand shot out and seized Jim by the back of the neck, fingers digging in agonizingly. Jim squirmed and tried to break free, but Kennart's grip was like the grasp of metal bands.

"Let go of me!" Jim bellowed. "We've got to save Chet! Let go! Do you hear?"

"He is dead," Kennart said mercilessly. "Do you wish to die, too?"

"We can still save him," Jim grunted. He lashed out at Kennart with his elbows, twisted, tried to land a solid blow. But the ice dweller held Jim at arm's length, fingers locked in place on Jim's neck.

133

Slowly, humiliatingly, with one arm alone, he forced him to his knees.

By this time, the others had come up, all but those in the sleds, who had halted abruptly when Chet vanished. Kennart released Jim, who got to his feet, glaring and rubbing his neck.

The fissure in the ice was completely closed now. There was no way of knowing where Chet had gone under.

Kennart said slowly, "He is gone, and we could not have saved him. The water draws the life from a man in moments. It sucks out the warmth. If you had gone to help him, Jim, you would have fallen through and been lost also. One death does not prevent the other. I am sorry if I angered you, but your life was in danger."

Jim did not answer. He stared in dull dismay at the treacherous ice. A hushed silence gripped the party. Ted Callison cracked his knuckles fiercely. Dr. Barnes shook his head in sadness.

"Is it safe to go on?" he asked.

Kennart nodded. "We must go on. It is dangerous here, but we will reach the open water safely. The ice has had the victim it demands."

Stunned, chilled by the tragedy, the voyagers pushed onward, forming their V once again. No more than ten minutes ago, Chet had been alive, striding along in his loose-jointed, long-legged way, perhaps thinking of fish he planned to catch the next time they stopped to rest. And now he bobbed lifeless beneath the ice, snuffed out in the flickering of an eye. They could not even put his body to rest. They could only mourn silently, and go on.

Up ahead, Kennart was walking carefully but at

134

his usual pace. Jim hesitated each time he put his foot down. The ice still seemed solid to him, but there might be other deadly traps waiting here, places where the ice was only paper-thin over a pocket of air, places where darkness might gleam suddenly out of the whiteness and claim a life.

Onward they went, detouring, zigzagging. Now it was Carl who walked to Jim's left; Roy and Ted made up the ends of the V, and Dr. Barnes had gone back to drive one of the sleds. Like the Dooney folk, the ice pack had claimed its toll.

They continued until the first shadows of night were falling. Their meal was a silent one that night, and no one spoke afterward. Jim slept badly, tossing and turning, eternally seeing the ice yawning to engulf Chet. It seemed to him as though they were moving across the skin of some giant creature, who might at any moment grow angered at them and destroy them with a shrug.

In the morning, they were on their way almost as soon as dawn had broken—once again, on foot, so that they covered only a few miles. But by midmorning Kennart told them they could return to the sleds. "The ice is stronger here," he said.

"How does he know?" Carl demanded, as they once more began to move at a fast pace. "Suppose he's wrong?"

"He's risking his own life as well as ours," Jim replied. "*He* isn't in any hurry to reach the sea. If he thinks it's safer here, it's because he's got good reason to think it."

When they stopped at noon, Kennart pointed toward the east, and said, "Tomorrow we will reach the sea. I give you my pledge of that."

"Then it wasn't impossible!" Jim said.

Kennart smiled distantly. "No," he said. "My father was mistaken. He said it could not be done, but he was wrong. It *can* be done. We will do it. Nothing is impossible. *Nothing!*"

# 11

## _Raiders of the Sea_

THE GOLDEN FIRE OF MIDDAY DANCED ACROSS THE FIELD
of ice. The sleds had halted, for they could go no
farther. Fifty yards ahead, the ice shield came to
an end. Beyond, a thousand ice floes bobbed and
drifted in the open water. Islands of ice, some of
them only a few feet across, others a hundred
yards or more in diameter, swirled, crashed
against one another, rose high out of the water for
a moment before falling back.

Jim walked as close to the edge of the ice field as
he dared, and looked out across the water.

The sea!

It was a stupefying sight. Where there had been

unending whiteness, now there was dark blue, stretching to the boundaries of the world. The wind swept low, blowing the surface of the water up into wavelets tipped with white caps of foam. Up off the sea came the salty breeze, cold but invigorating. Jim felt faintly dazed by the thought of such a bulk of water lying in their path.

"Here we wait," Kennart said. "The Sea People will come ashore along this coast."

"How long will it be?" Dr. Barnes asked.

Kennart shook his head and grinned, showing gleaming white teeth. "A day," he said. "Or six days, or twenty. Who knows the way of the Sea People? But they come here. They sail past, and put men ashore to hunt."

It seemed like madness, Jim thought—to camp here by the edge of the sea, waiting for the landing of seafarers who might put in to shore anywhere within a thousand miles. But he knew they had no choice. They could not contact the Sea People. And Kennart had agreed to wait with them. He would not leave them, he said, until he saw them safely to sea.

They waited.

It was not the most comforting place in the world to camp. The ice seemed sturdy enough, here, but every now and then a vast chunk would crack free of the ice shelf and go drifting out into the open water. Late on the day of their arrival, an ice mass at least a hundred feet in diameter broke away on a voyage of its own. But Kennart didn't seem troubled. So long as they all stayed together, it did not appear really to matter whether they remained on the mainland or went bobbing off on a little ice-floe island. The seafarers, he said, would find them all the same. If he were worried about his own return trip, he kept those worries out of sight.

On the second day the cry went up: "A sail! A sail! They're coming!"

Jim looked out to sea. It was a thrilling sight: a ship coming down from the north, sailing parallel to the shore, weaving is way riskily between the butting, rearing floes of ice. The ship was bigger than Jim had expected, more than a hundred feet long, its hull made of wood planks painted a bright red. A sail of black cloth bellied in the breeze. On the ship's prow a fearsome figurehead was carved: a dragon's neck, ending in a grisly head whose eyes were glittering yellow, whose savage teeth looked like wolf teeth mounted in the wood.

Through the binoculars, Jim could make out figures moving aboard the ship—husky men clad in leather doublets, brawny figures with long hair, long beards.

"They see us," Carl said. "They're putting in toward shore."

"How can they reach it?" Jim asked. "They'll be caved in by the floating islands of ice."

Kennart laughed. "They know their trade," he said quietly. "They will have no trouble."

He was right. With magnificent ease, the ship found a path through the floating ice, gliding gracefully in until it was within a dozen yards of shore. Crewmen appeared at the bow and threw down anchors. The seafarers' ship rode superbly in the water, ice snapping at its hull but unable to harm it.

A ladder of animal hide was lowered. The seven men on the shore waited silently as the seafarers came ashore, marching down their hinged wooden gangplank.

They came armed. They carried spears and daggers of bone, and short swords slung at their waists. A dozen of them left the ship, swaggering and bold, their faces set in harsh, unfriendly lines. Eight of the twelve were red-haired men. Their fiery manes and beards blazed in the midday sun. They filed ashore and arrayed themselves in a line, backs to the sea.

One of them, the biggest and most fearsome, snapped something in an unfamiliar language studded with clicking consonants and broad vowels. Not a word was intelligible, but the meaning was clear enough: the seafarer wanted to know who the travelers were, and by what right they came here?

"They speak not our tongue," Kennart whispered. "I will address them in theirs."

He stepped forward. Adopting an expression every bit as arrogant as that of the man who faced him, Kennart made reply, spitting the words out as though it soiled his lips to have to utter such barbaric jargon.

There was a long, crackling silence when Kennart finished speaking. Then the seafarer chief uttered a single syllable.

Kennart turned red. He replied with two short, violent bursts of words, the sounds tumbling over one another as they emerged. It was the turn of the Sea People to grow hot with anger. They stirred menacingly, hands stealing to the hilts of their swords. Aboard the ship, dozens of bearded faces peered down, taking it all in.

An argument was raging now. Voices were growing heated. Kennart said something, only to be shouted down by the sea-chief, and to shout the bearded one down in turn. The situation looked critical. Standing by the sled, Jim eyed a power torch, readying himself to grab it if matters came to a boil. But what would they do, he wondered, if there were a battle? They needed the co-operation of these Sea People, not their enmity.

The negotiations seemed to have broken down. Kennart turned, talked back to the tense group by the sleds. Scratching his chin thoughtfully, Kennart said, "It happens that they make voyage now to the far side of the ice. But they are not eager for passengers. They like not your looks, men of New York."

"Our looks don't matter," Dr. Barnes said. "What will they take as fee to carry us? What do they need?"

"Nothing you can give them," Kennart said. "There the trouble lies. The Sea People need only food from the shore, and that you cannot offer."

"Are there sick men aboard?" Dr. Barnes asked. "We can try to heal them. We have medicines with us."

Kennart returned and parleyed again with the seafarer's chief. This time, the conversation was less heated; it seemed that the man of the sea was replying with irony now rather than with anger. For long moments they talked. Then Kennart walked back to the sleds.

"He asked me why your faces were so pale," Kennart reported. "I told him you had come up out of the ice from a city in the Earth, and he laughed at me. He did not believe me. I told him of your journey, and said that the gods protected you,

141

but he laughed at that, too. His gods are not mine. He said he has no sick men on board, no need of passengers, no wish to take you. He is half minded, he says, to kill you for the sport, and take your sleighs to sell to the people of the South."

"Friendly sort," Jim muttered.

Dr. Barnes said, "Isn't there any way we can buy a trip across? Anything we can give him?"

Kennart smiled crookedly. "He said one thing, I think as a joke. He said if any of you can vanquish him in single combat, he will grant you passage. Otherwise he will take your lives. It is his way of amusing himself."

"Impossible," Dr. Barnes said. "We couldn't—"

"Wait, Dad," Jim cut in. He glanced at Kennart and said, "Tell him I accept his challenge, but I demand my choice of weapons."

Kennart frowned. Dr. Barnes said, "What are you up to, Jim?"

"Leave this to me, Dad."

"You can't duel with that viking! He'll cut you to shreds, Jim! He must weigh almost three hundred pounds, and—"

"I'll handle him," Jim said. "Go on, Kennart. Tell him I accept."

"I forbid this, Jim," Dr. Barnes said.

Jim looked steadily at his father. "I think I can handle this, Dad. It's our only chance to get across. If they don't take us, we're stranded here at the edge of the sea—provided they don't kill us outright. Give me the chance. Kennart's father didn't stop *him*. You're *our* chief. Let me do what I want to do."

Dr. Barnes frowned uncertainly. He did not reply.

But Kennart, as though grasping something that Jim's father could not or would not see, was already on his way back to the waiting sea-chief, who stood with folded arms, smiling coldly. They talked. Then Kennart turned.

"He is amused," Kennart reported. "But he says he accepts, and wants to know your choice of weapons. Sword, spear, or dagger?"

"None of those," Jim answered. "Tell him I'll fight him with bare hands!"

Kennart's eyes widened. He said. "Now you joke, too?"

"Bare hands!" Jim repeated.

Kennart spoke, and the sea-chief broke into gales of laughter, roaring and stamping his feet in a way that threatened to buckle the entire ice shelf. His men were laughing, too, and one of them called up to the sailors on board the ship, who responded with hearty guffaws.

Among the group of New Yorkers, though, there was no laughter. Dr. Barnes nodded at Jim, understanding at last.

Kennart said to Jim, "He wants to know, is it to death you fight?"

Jim said, "Tell him we'll fight until one of us admits defeat. There's no need to fight to death."

Kennart spoke again. The sea-chief answered.

Kennart said, "He agrees. He says, let the battle begin!"

The two groups formed a circle on the ice, the New Yorkers ranged by their sleds, the Sea People along the water's edge. Between them was an open space forty feet across. Jim moved out into the open, and waited.

The sea-chief was divesting himself of his sword and dagger, of his heavy outer coat of fur-trimmed leather. Jim, too, took off his outer coat. The temperature was above freezing, and he would need all the mobility he could summon.

Jim was accustomed to this sort of combat —though never before had he fought for stakes like these. In the underground city, one had to keep in shape, or the body would rot, muscles sagging into shapelessness. Each level of New York had its own gymnasium, and there the citizens swam and exercised. An hour a day was compulsory until the age of sixteen; after that, it was a voluntary matter, but few neglected it. Jim had learned fencing in the gymnasium, and he had fair skill at it. But he did not trust himself against the sea captain's sword. Jim had other arts. He had learned wrestling from a master, and each year since boyhood had won medals in the city tournaments. His lean figure did not ripple with muscle, but his judo skill compensated for that. Long hours of practice had made Jim a cunning fighter. His skills had served him well enough against the chieftain of the Dooney folk. Would they be sufficient now?

The combatants faced each other. Jim was perhaps an inch taller than the chief of the Sea People, but gave away nearly a hundred pounds. The sea-chief was massive, with arms thicker than Jim's legs, and legs whose thews bulged incredibly. It seemed as though he was twice Jim's breadth through the shoulders. Jim looked fragile, helpless against the older man. A sudden breeze might blow Jim away, or so it appeared to the onlookers. The muscles of the sea-chief swelled

144

under the thin leather tunic. His red hair and flaming beard tossed in the wind. Jim, red-haired also, waited for the other to advance.

The chief rumbled something whose meaning unmistakably was, "I'm going to break you in little pieces, boy!"

Then he came ponderously forward.

Jim did not move until the bulky captain was almost upon him. He stared straight into the fierce green eyes, and felt the ice shake as the big man pounded it. Two huge calloused hands reached for Jim. He let the hands actually touch his shoulders, then unexpectedly leaned back, falling away and to the side. The chief grunted in surprise, arms pinwheeling.

Jim deftly broke his own fall, pivoted, grabbed one of the thick wrists. The sea captain was already toppling forward, off balance, and Jim levered against the ice, applying thrust in the direction the big man was going. His foot swept across the chieftain's shins, completing the job of upending him.

The effect was impressive. The sea-chief's legs went out from under him, and he fell belly-first, dealing the ice a slam such as nearly shattered it. He went skidding ten feet and came to a halt. Jim did not follow.

There was murder in the captain's eye as he got to his feet. He extended his hands like two clutching claws and came charging toward Jim, rumbling in anger.

This time Jim did not fall away. He sidestepped, feinted as though to go under the big man's left arm, swung around rapidly, and seized his opponent's right arm instead. Jim gasped as a balled fist

145

smashed into his side, but followed through all the same, delicately twisting the right arm against its own axis. The chief spun around, helpless, his left arm flailing, and as he tried to keep Jim from breaking the right one altogether, Jim was able to ease himself into a leverage position for an overhead fling.

A moment later the chief of the Sea People was soaring through the air, flipping over Jim's head and coming down with a sound like that of thunder against the ice.

There was a deadly silence. The chief was slower to get up this time. Jim stood poised, panting, his side aching where the fist had struck him. He knew that if those monstrous fists ever hit home solidly, the fight would be over in that instant. But he was faster than the chief, and also a good deal smarter.

A third time the big man approached his unpredictable adversary. He circled warily, uneasy about charging again. His hands clawed air; he seemed to be hoping that Jim would take the offensive and come within reach of a crushing hug. Jim had no such idea, though. He waited patiently. He who lost patience first was going to end second best in this struggle.

The chief snarled and spat. His eyes flashed defiance. He moved toward Jim, lifting his arms high overhead. As he began to bring them down, Jim darted in, jabbed the big man playfully in the belly with the side of his hand to draw a grunt, then chopped sharply against the chief's biceps. It was like chopping against a stone wall, but the shot had its effect. The chief pulled the injured

146

arm in toward his side. Jim quickly slammed a second edge-on shot against the chief's funny bone.

The big man howled in agony. With his left hand, he swatted at Jim as though trying to dipose of an irritating insect. It was a mistake. Jim caught the hand as it swung toward him, jerked it down and then up, did a little dance, and ended with the chief's arm doubled behind the massive body.

"Down," Jim ordered. "Down or I'll break it right off!"

The chief did not understand the words, but the idea got plainly across all the same. After a tentative, experimental attempt to break Jim's hold had shown him that any motion would only increase the pressure on his arm, the big man sank angrily to his knees.

"Good boy," Jim said. "Now farther. Kiss the ice."

He levered upward on the tortured arm. The chief bent toward the ice. His beard brushed it. His lips touched it. Jim heard the men of the sea muttering, whispering among themselves. Slowly he eased the big man upward and waited for an admission of defeat.

No admission came. The chief tensed, wary but stubborn.

Jim looked at Kennart. "Tell him I'll break his arm if he doesn't give up! Tell him the fight's all over!"

Kennart said something. The chief growled a reply.

Kennart said, "He doesn't give ground! He says he'll fight even with a broken arm!"

Jim had never met with a situation like that. He maintained the grip, tightening it a little, but never before had anyone dared him to go ahead and break his arm. Jim couldn't do it. So far as he was concerned, the fight was over right now. Did the chief plan to fight to the death anyway?

"Tell him I release him," Jim called to Kennart. "Tell him I claim victory."

"Better not," Kennart warned. "If you let go of him—"

Jim discovered what would happen even before Kennart got the words out. He started to slacken his grip, and the chief began to rise, already swinging around with his free hand to take a swipe at Jim.

"Sorry," Jim said. "I don't want to do this, but some people are stubborn as stone."

He put theory into practice. A gentle nudge and a twist and the chief boomed in pain. Jim had merely dislocated his shoulder, instead of breaking his arm.

Left arm dangling limply, the chief returned to the attack. Perspiration beaded his face now, and his hair was pasted to his forehead. Wild, berserk, he clubbed at Jim, howled at him, begged him in wordless shrieks to hold still and be killed. Jim danced around him, annoyed with the obstinate barbarian for prolonging the fight this way.

The chief lurched suddenly and swung his good arm in a curving arc. Jim leaned toward him, expecting to catch the arm and send the chief flying once again, but the power of that ponderous arm fooled him. An instant later Jim found himself caught, trapped by the arm, crushed up against the chief's body. He felt his ribs rubbing together. The air rushed from his lungs. Jim gasped for breath, cursing his overconfidence, wondering if he would ever get free. The maddened chief might very well crush him to death before he let go.

Jim strained. He spread his shoulders, struggled with all his might. No use. He was choking, his face going purple, his eyes bulging.

Then he found a way. He bowed his head, slammed it up with all his might into the seachief's long chin!

The bearded man's head went shooting back. He began to stumble, and had to let go of Jim, who took every advantage of his regained freedom. Seizing the madly waving arm, Jim ran round, slid the big man across the ice a few feet, then levered him into the air!

He soared high, higher than the last time . . .

And crashed with booming impact. He landed and went skittering like a doll across the ice, coming to rest only a few feet from his own men.

Jim stood his ground, filling his lungs gratefully with air and trying to recover from that crushing bear hug, which had left him faint and dizzy. The next time, he told himself, he would not be so merciful about dislocating arms when he was in a position to break them.

But there was no next time. Long moments passed, and still the great form lay sprawled on the ice like some whale beached by the tides. None of his men dared approach him. They stood in a tight knot, stunned, bewildered by his downfall.

Finally the big man sat up. He shook his head as though to clear cobwebs from it, and looked down at his dangling arm. He moved it experimentally, winced, looked at Kennart, and muttered something in a low, barely audible voice.

Kennart said to Jim, "He admits defeat. He says you may come as passengers on his ship. But there is a condition." Kennart grinned. "He wishes you to teach him how you fought like that!"

# 12

## *The Horizon Draws Near*

WITH KENNART SERVING AS INTERPRETER, THE JOB OF
getting the sleds aboard the ship moved more
smoothly than the New Yorkers expected. Twenty
sailors descended from the vessel which rocked
gently at anchor as they maneuvered the bulky
sleds up and into the hold. The chief, still glower-
ing over his defeat, supervised the maneuver.

Jim called Kennart aside. "Tell him," he said,
"that we have a healer among us who can restore
his shoulder. Tell him that I hope he will hold no
anger at me for his defeat."

Kennart carried the message. The chief grunted

a reply, and Kennart said, "Send him your healer. He says he is angry not at you but at himself."

Carl went to the chief, and employed his meager first-aid training to deal with the dislocation. He simply seized the shoulder and firmly forced it back into place, a process that must have been horribly painful, but which drew not a whimper from the patient.

Soon all was in readiness for departure. The sleds and their contents had been loaded, and nothing remained but to climb the ladder and go on board.

Jim realized with a pang of sadness that the time of parting from Kennart had come. The fair-haired man stood alone on the shore, watching quietly. He had traveled with them a week; he had risked his life to guide them, and he had become one of them, for all his difference of background. He had been a friend, and friends were not easily come by in this frigid world.

"I wish you could come with us," Jim said.

"So, too, do I," Kennart replied. "But tasks await me. I have people who depend on me. I can go no farther."

"Is there any way we can thank you?"

Kennart smiled. "Not with gifts, Jim. You are still my guest, and I will take no gift of you. Except perhaps for the secret of hurling a huge man like a toy. Can you tell me how it is done?"

"It takes long training," Jim said with a laugh and a shake of the head. "I could teach you, yes—as fast as you could teach me how to cross the ice in safety."

"I understand," the other said. "Well, then. We come to the parting. I wish you fair voyage. And if ever you pass this way again, I bid you search us out."

"We will do that," Jim promised.

Kennart said good-by to each man in turn, while the seafarers hoisted their anchors. Jim clambered aboard the ship; Carl and Roy followed him. No one remained on shore, now, but Kennart, alone against a field of white.

The ship put out for sea. Jim remained at the rail a long time, staring at the dwindling figure on the shelf of ice. And then, at last, Kennart was lost to sight, and Jim turned away, silently wishing the brave Jersey a safe journey home.

After a day aboard ship, Jim decided that he very much preferred sledding over thin ice. Every pulse, every heave of the sea translated itself directly into a rolling motion underfoot. The crewmen, raised from childhood to this way of life, moved about with confidence and ease, smirking at the six unhappy landlubbers who clung grimly to the supports.

The ship was a floating village, Jim soon found. Down below were women and children, busy at tasks of their own. With so many dozens of people crammed aboard the vessel, privacy was unknown; no one had more than a couple of square feet to himself. The six passengers had been installed right on deck, near the stern; cold sea spray washed over them constantly, until they pitched their tents in self-defense.

It was not a comfortable journey. But the New York men had not asked for comfort, merely for a way across the open water. That, they were getting. The vessel slipped speedily through the sea, sailors working in shifts through day and night to make the most of the strong wind out of the west. Time blurred. There was nothing for the passengers to do aboard ship, since they could not speak a word to any of the seafarers, had no duties, and were too seasick most of the time to read or play time-passing games with one another. On, on, endlessly eastward they moved, the sea growing now choppy, now calm. Floating islands of ice drifted past. In places the ice floes were thick and numerous, and it seemed as though they might be approaching the far shore; but then the water cleared again, and nothing but open water stretched before them.

It developed that the seafarers' chief had been serious about wanting to learn the secrets of Jim's wrestling mastery. On a day of calm sea, he called for a demonstration, indicating by signs that Jim should teach them his art. Jim was amused to see that the chief himself did not come forward to take part in the demonstration. He sent in his stead a brawny young giant who towered half a head over Jim. Jim heard the chief saying something to his men, and it was easy enough to guess what it was: "I wish to watch and see how he does it," the chief was probably declaring, to conceal his unwillingness to have a second humiliation at Jim's hands.

Everyone who could be spared from duty gathered round to watch. Even some of the women peeped up from below decks. Jim's new adversary was no older than Jim, and just as fast on his feet, and twice as strong. But his only idea of wrestling was to lock his arms around his opponent and hug him to death. Again and again, the big fellow charged Jim, only to wind up slamming back-first into the hard deck. Bloody but unbowed, he picked himself up and tried again, and again, and again. He never seemed to catch on. Always, when he charged, there was an arm jutting out that could be caught, and deftly twisted, and used as a lever to send him flying. He didn't seem to understand that Jim was capitalizing on his momentum —that the harder he charged, the harder he was going to get slammed.

The "demonstration" lasted half an hour. Jim displayed his whole repertoire, the arm locks and back locks and flips and twists and parries. By the time the chief finally broke it up, Jim had worked up a hearty sweat but hadn't been hurt at all, and his victim was sullenly nursing an assortment of bruises and bone jars that he'd feel for a week.

Later, Jim saw some of the sailors practicing judo holds on each other. It was a comic sight. They were trying to be agile, trying hard to imitate Jim's use of leverage and momentum, but they just didn't have the knack. Somehow they invariably ended up gripping each other's wrists and swinging round and round in a wild, clumsy, foolish-looking dance.

"No," Jim told them. "You've got to get your *body* behind it. Like this. Imagine that you're a whip, and you're cracking like a pistol shot—"

Of course, they were unable to understand what he was telling them. He pantomimed it for them, and they smiled and nodded and went at it again, but as before they grabbed wrists and swung violently until it seemed both combatants would go flying off into the sea.

155

"Don't let it discourage you," Jim told them. "I looked just as silly, at first. It takes years of practice."

While Jim tried in vain to teach the sailors judo, Ted Callison was busy with the radio. He and Jim's father huddled for long hours over the set, trying to pick up London. They made contact, finally, and let the Londoners know that they were still in for a visit. London seemed surprised that the New York party had been able to travel so far in safety. Only two casualties out of eight, in several weeks of journeying, and the hardest part of the trip behind them. . . .

"They're going to send a party out to meet us," Dr. Barnes reported. "We're going to try to make rendezvous with them somewhere on the European ice shelf."

That ice shelf grew daily nearer. There were delays, twice, when schools of dolphins came near the ship, and the seafarers put down boats of harpooners to take the prizes. Jim watched in awe as the sleek creatures sped by, and was equally impressed with the skill of the muscular harpooners. He thought of Chet, and how he would have loved to see the dolphins. Those nights, they fed on fresh meat.

Then came a day of storm at sea, and a thick band of cloud descended, fogging them in. Cold rain pelted down, and lightning flashed in the heavens, and the muffled boom of thunder rolled across the waters. The ship tossed wildly, while sailors ran to and fro and the six passengers kept to their deckside tents. It seemed as though they could never survive the fury of the storm, as though they were fated to end at the bottom of the icy sea after having come so far. Great slabs of drifting ice pounded at the hull like the hammers of giants, and the ship veered perilously, high waves crashing across the bow and sending cold water sluicing over the deck.

Toward midnight the storm relented. Almost miraculously, the fog cleared, and the rain turned to snow, and the sea calmed. Overhead gleamed the moon, haloed by a cloud. White, fluffy flakes drifted down, glittering like tinsel in the night, and lost themselves in the sea. It was a scene of pure magic, as tranquil and delicate as the storm had been violent and tempestuous. Chilled and wet through, teeth chattering, Jim stood by the rail a long moment, looking moonward.

Day slid into day, and one day there was the flash of wings; the sound of mocking laughter on high, and gulls swept past and out to sea, soaring splendidly on the wind. Excitement spurred the passengers. Jim followed the birds with the field glasses until they were lost to view.

"We're nearing shore," Ted declared. "We must be. The crewmen are all pointing at the birds."

"Look at them!" Jim cried. "Look at them soar!"

Ted nodded. As always, his blunt, high-cheekboned face displayed little emotion. "They're pretty, aren't they?" he said in a matter-of-fact voice.

"They're marvelous," Jim said. "Look! Here come some more!"

Another flight of gulls sliced past, cresting the ship only feet from the sailtops, filling the air with

157

their wild screeching. They, too, sped past, swirling downward to the water to harvest their lunch. Then they were gone.

Jim turned. The sailors, those fierce, red-bearded men, had gathered together on the fore-deck, and stood with bowed heads while their captain intoned a series of short lines of verse. Even in the harsh seafarer language, the words sounded oddly beautiful. The ceremony lasted perhaps five minutes, and ended when a young crewman came forward carrying a slab of dried meat.

The captain hurled it into the sea. Then the assembly broke up. Its meaning was obvious: the sailors had been giving thanks for a safe crossing, and were making a gratitude offering to the god of the waters.

Late that afternoon, the shore of Europe came into sight.

A thin line of white rimmed the horizon. Ice floes clustered, thick in the water. Occasionally some gleaming, powerful creature could be seen, gliding through the water or sunning itself on a little island of ice—a walrus, perhaps, or a seal. Sea birds were common here, wheeling and shrieking overhead. The scene was much the same as that which they had left behind the day they parted with Kennart. A wide, flat sheet of ice stretched before them.

The vessel of the seafarers came to "port," anchoring against the ice shelf itself, and the sleds were lowered from the ship. One by one, the New Yorkers disembarked. As Jim started to go down the ladder, the seafarer chieftain suddenly came up to him, reached out, took his hand.

158

The bearded captain's grip was bone-crushing. Jim endured it, gritting his teeth. The big man smiled, drew close to Jim, pounded him playfully on the back. The stink of salt fish came from him, and Jim fought for breath.

"Sure," Jim said, grinning back. "I understand. You have no hard feelings."

The chief said something in his incomprehensible language.

"Thanks," Jim said. "And I hope you have a safe voyage, too, wherever you're going. But I wish you'd let go of my hand. I may need it again."

The chief said something else, and released him. Jim smiled, clapped the bulky captain stoutly on the shoulder—the good one, not the one he had dislocated—and scrambled down the ladder before the seafarer could find some other equally strenuous way to show his friendship. Jim flexed his fingers as he left the ship. Nothing broken, he thought. Only bent, a little.

When all was unloaded, the seafarers raised anchor, lifted sail. They waved, shouted raucous farewells, as their ship began to glide off, southward along the ice shore.

"They aren't such bad sorts at all," Carl said.

"Just a bit roughhewn," Jim commented. "But friendly, once you get to know them."

Dr. Barnes came over. "We're going to start out right away," he said. "Unless anyone has any objections."

"How far do you figure we are from London, Dad?" Jim asked.

The older man shook his head. "About a thousand miles, I'd guess. Just exactly how far, I can't say. Dave is going to run some readings later on in

159

the day. One thing's certain: we're well past the halfway point."

That was good news, Jim thought. If more lay behind them than ahead, there was no reason why they could not make it the rest of the way to London.

But he felt little jubilation at the thought. For two of those who had started out from New York, the trip had long since ended. Others might yet lose their lives before London was attained. And no one could predict the welcome they would get when finally they reached their long-sought goal. Right now, however, simply the hope of getting to London was enough to spur them on through hardship and danger. But if they reached London, and were turned away? Where to then? Back across the ice and sea to New York? No, that was impossible.

Jim preferred to think little of such things. There was time to confront trouble when it came to plague them; no need to fret ahead of time.

The sleds were fully charged. The six voyagers spent a while getting accustomed to *terra firma* again, to an environment that remained steady beneath their feet, and then they were off, once again journeying toward the sunrise.

This part of the ice pack was much like that which lay between the Jersey encampment and the sea. But they had no Kennart to guide them now, and could only trust to luck that they would avoid the snares and pitfalls of the ice. There was no sign of human life here, no abandoned igloos, no traces of nomad hunters. Animal tracks in the light covering of snow above the ice told of wildlife, but no creatures appeared.

Their luck was good. The ice was sturdy here, and no perils presented themselves. Their first day on the European ice shelf was the best they had had since leaving New York; they covered more than a hundred miles coursing eastward in the encouraging knowledge that with each passing mile they were that much farther from the sea, that much closer to the solid ice that overlay the land ahead.

Ted was in constant contact with London, now. Here, in easy radio range, the London signal came in clear and sharp. A party had left the underground city, they learned, and was heading westward to meet them. The intended rendezvous was the glacier above what once had been the emerald isle of Ireland, and the Londoners provided crisp directions for the meeting.

"It sounds as if they've been out of their city before," Ted remarked. "They seem to know their way around on the ice fields."

"Maybe they don't have the same taboo about the surface that New York has," Jim suggested. "It's a good sign, anyway, I'd say."

"But they don't sound very friendly," Dr. Barnes said, half to himself. "They're always so suspicious, so bristly."

"They're coming to meet us, aren't they?" Roy Veeder said. "That indicates they have friendly intentions."

"Does it?" Dr. Barnes demanded.

The question seemed to hang like a wraith in the frosty air. *Does it?* Jim wondered about that. Did sending a party mean a desire for friendship—or simply a wish to intercept the New Yorkers before they penetrated very far into Europe?

They would know, soon enough.

Continuing onward, they encountered their first Europeans late on the third day—a band of primitive-looking people engaged in skinning a gigantic moose. Skin-clad, squat and hairy, they reminded Jim of the moose hunters they had met thousands of miles to the west, the simple folk who had so easily been awed by Carl's medical skills. These, though, were even more readily cowed. The moose-hunting nomads of the earlier incident had been ready to fight the strangers, at least at first. But these people took one look at the two weird sleds advancing toward them over the ice and fled, screaming and stampeding.

"Come back!" the New Yorkers yelled. "We aren't going to hurt you!"

The shouts only redoubled the panic of the fleeing nomads. They ran desperately, as though the devil were on their tail, and in moments they had vanished from sight.

"They left their kill behind," Dave Ellis said.

Ted Callison laughed heartily. "We eat fresh meat tonight, then!"

"It doesn't belong to us," Roy argued.

Ted shrugged. "It's ours by right of discovery. They aren't coming back for it. They're probably still running, as a matter of fact. I say we eat it and let them kill another moose when they stop running."

Dr. Barnes said, "Ted's right. If we leave a half-dressed carcass here, it'll attract wolves. We'll take what we want, and bury the rest under the ice."

That evening they feasted. Squatting around their fire, they devoured roast moose as gaily as though it were an everyday meal for them. Jim wondered what the good folks of New York City would say if they could look upon the scene. Six men, weather-beaten and shabby, tanned by sun and wind, unshaven cheeks covered with the coarse stubble of sprouting beards, sitting around a campfire in twenty-degree weather, munching like savages on chewy chunks of half-cooked meat! They had traveled a long distance—and not merely in miles—from the antiseptic, orderly, underground city, with its never-changing mild temperature and its efficient cafeterias dishing out scientifically calculated portions of synthetic protein!

But there was a price for their return to the older ways of mankind. Jim lay sound asleep that night, dreaming that he was still aboard the rolling, pitching ship, teaching judo to long-bearded vikings, when a hand shook him into wakefulness.

He stirred reluctantly. "Who—what—?" He looked up at the stocky figure of Ted Callison. "Hey, what is this?" Jim demanded sleepily. "I stood watch already tonight! You've got the wrong guy!"

"I'm waking everybody up," Ted said. "There's an emergency!"

"Huh?"

"It's Roy," Ted said. "He's sick. He's burning up with fever. We've got to do something for him!"

163

# 13

## *Chilly Welcome*

ROY LAY GROANING IN A FAR CORNER OF THE TENT. HIS face was white as the snow outside, and gleamed with perspiration. Eyes closed, lips drawn back in agony, he writhed and clutched at his body. Carl and Dr. Barnes knelt over him. Carl stared into his medic kit as though hoping to find a magic wand in it. His slender medical skills did not encompass such things as this.

"High fever," Dr. Barnes muttered. "He's delirious. Carl, does that kit of yours have anything to help?"

Carl shrugged. "There's some medicine, but it's not much. Headache tablets, mostly."

Roy stirred. His eyes opened, but they were glassy, and saw nothing. "Snow," he whispered, croaking harshly. "Lie down in the snow. Cool off. Cool . . ."

"Easy, there," Dr. Barnes said. "You'll be all right soon, Roy. We've got medicine for you."

"Burning," Roy said. "*Burning!*"

"Try this," Carl said. He took a spray tube from the medic kit. "It's marked for infection and swelling. At least it can't hurt him. Should I?"

"Go ahead," Dr. Barnes said.

Carl held the spray tube to Roy's arm, and pressed the stud. There was a tiny buzzing sound as the ultrasonic needle drove the medicine through Roy's skin, into the vein. Roy took no notice. He continued to twist, to mutter.

Methodically, Carl searched through the scant medical equipment the expedition possessed. Nothing seemed to be of any use. He had equipment to guard against infection, to close a wound, to stop bleeding. But there was nothing that could break a fever. Roy sweltered on. Carl took his temperature and looked up solemnly. "It's a hundred and five," he said. "He's really on fire!"

The groans grew more intense. Stifling in the closeness of the tent, Jim stepped outside into the chill. Ted Callison followed him, and, a moment later, Dave Ellis.

Ted shook his head pessimistically. "We're going to lose him," he said.

"No!" Jim snapped. "He's just got a fever, that's all!"

"That's all? He's got a bacterial infection. He must have picked something up from that meat we ate tonight. We aren't protected against the germs

165

they have up here. It's a miracle we haven't all come down with something by this time."

Jim shook his head doggedly. "All right, so he's got a high fever. Haven't you ever had a fever? It hasn't killed you, has it?"

"This is different. The bug that's in Roy is something we have no immunity against. It'll sweep right through him and burn him out."

The groans from within the tent grew louder. There was no sleep for any of them, the rest of that night.

And then—shortly before dawn—came silence.

They moved on after burying Roy, hardly bothering about a breakfast meal. His death had shaken everyone, and that day no one spoke a word that was not strictly necessary.

Death came swiftly in this harsh upper world, Jim thought, and it came without warning. In the snug retreat below the ice, there were no accidents, no dangers, almost no diseases. An eighty-year lifespan was only commonplace in New York; people lived on past the century mark, on for a hundred ten, a hundred twenty years sometimes, dying only when the worn-out body could at last no longer sustain life.

Not here. Here death engulfed you when you least expected it. A lucky spear thrust by an outraged barbarian chief; a sudden opening and closing of the ice; an insidious germ that took you in the aftermath of a robust meal. Jim shivered. For all he knew, the seeds of what had killed Roy with such swiftness were ripening within them all, and before another dawn they would all lie dead or dying in the snow.

But no one else developed the fever. The victim

had been claimed, and the rest were spared for another day. By nightfall, a hundred miles lay between Roy's grave and their camp. The ice field was beginning a gentle upgrade that told them they were passing from the frozen sea onto the glacier-locked land, and that was a comfort.

After dark, Ted picked up London on the radio, and heard that the expeditionary party London had sent out was nearing them steadily.

Just before noon the next day, the Londoners came into view.

It was possible to see them far off, a dark line in the distance. On the flat waste of the ice plateau, nothing barred the view for miles in any direction, and the Londoners were plain to see.

"They have sleds, too," Jim said. "Look how fast they're moving!"

"And there seem to be plenty of them," Ted muttered. "They didn't send an expedition, they sent an army!"

Half an hour more, and the two groups had come together.

The Londoners had already halted. Their sleds —five of them—were drawn up in a curving line across the ice, and men waited, arms folded, for the New Yorkers to approach. It was a moment that made history, Jim thought—the first face-to-face contact between a city of Europe and one of North America in hundreds of years.

"They're a grim bunch," Dave Ellis said. "Not a smile among them!"

"We've faced worse than this and come out alive," Ted told him. "At least these people are civilized!"

"They're the worst kind, don't you know?" Carl said with a jaunty grin.

The waiting Londoners seemed somehow menacing. They were clad well, in thick protective wraps, and their hair, worn oddly long, gave them something of a barbaric look. But their pale faces and soft skin told of their city heritage. They were armed, too—not with power torches, apparently, but with small arms holstered at their hips.

The five New Yorkers advanced until they were a few yards from the Londoners. Dr. Barnes left the sled and went forward, one hand upraised in welcome.

"Greetings from New York!" he boomed.

A Londoner detached himself from the group and approached. He was a slab-jawed, gray-eyed man, who bore himself with obvious self-satisfaction. Nodding to Dr. Barnes, he said, "Who are you, New Yorker?"

"Raymond Barnes. And you?"

"John Moncrieff. Captain, London Constabulary Patrol."

"A policeman?"

"A soldier," Moncrieff said frostily. He signaled to one of his men. "Pitch a tent," he ordered. To Dr. Barnes he said, "I want to talk to you and your second-in-command. The others can wait outside."

"I have no second-in-command," Dr. Barnes replied evenly. "In our group we are all equals."

"Pick one," Moncrieff said. "I'll talk to only two of you, no more. I can't abide a rabble!"

"Five is no rabble," Dr. Barnes retorted. "Whatever you have to say to us, you can say to all of us."

Moncrieff scowled and shook his head. "Don't

168

be obstinate, New Yorker! You're on Londoner territory now. Be wary and make no quarrels. I'll talk to two of you."

Dr. Barnes flung his shoulders high, as though to say this was too trivial a point to feud over. Almost at random, he pointed to Ted Callison and aid, "All right, Ted. You come with me. Jim, Dave, Carl —I'm sorry. One of us has to give in."

The tent was up. Ted, Dr. Barnes, Moncrieff, and a couple of other Londoners went within, and the flap was closed. The rest of the Londoners remained in guarded, tense postures, eyeing the three New Yorkers with mingled fear and hostility.

"What are they so jumpy about?" Carl asked. "It wouldn't cost them anything to be friendlier."

"They're like most of the people in New York," Jim said. "Suspicious of anything new. We're strangers. We come from another city. They don't know what to make of us, and they're not going to relax one bit."

Some of the Londoners, though, seemed unabashedly curious about the New Yorkers. One in particular, after studying Jim with unconcealed fascination for a long moment, finally made so bold as to come over and speak to him.

"Hello, there. What's your name?"

"Jim Barnes."

"I'm Colin Thornton." The Londoner looked young, certainly still in his teens. He stood stiffly upright, but he was short and could not hide the fact. He was sturdy, though, with a wide-shouldered frame. Long soft brown hair tumbled across his forehead and nearly into his dark eyes. He stared at Jim and said, "How old are you?"

"Seventeen."

"So am I. You look older than that."

"I need a shave," Jim said with a laugh. "I've been too busy to bother with such things lately."

Colin seemed full of questions. "How long have you been in the army?" he shot at Jim.

"I'm not in the army."

"You're not? Then what do you do in New York?"

"I go to school," Jim said. "At least, I *went* to school. I was studying to be a hydroponics engineer."

"We have those, too," Colin said. "But I wouldn't want to be one. I joined the army when I was thirteen. How big an army does New York have?"

"We don't have an army."

"You're joking me, New Yorker!"

"It's the truth. What does a city need an army for, under the glacier? We've got police, though. Carl, over there, was a policeman."

"Aren't you afraid of invaders?" Colin asked.

"There's a mile of ice between New York and the surface. We don't worry about invasions. Does London get raided often?"

Colin scuffed at the snow. "The barbarians came down the tunnel about thirty years ago," he said. "We killed them all, but they gave us a time. Since then we've had an army." The dark, glittering eyes scanned Jim suddenly. "You don't carry a gun either, do you?"

"No. I don't."

"No weapons at all?"

"We have weapons," Jim said, not wanting to tell the Londoner too much. "But not guns. Not like yours."

"Want to see my gun?"

"If you don't mind showing it."

"Why should I mind?" Colin asked.

"I don't know. You Londoners all seem so suspicious. Perhaps you wouldn't care to let me see your gun."

"I'll let you see. Here."

Colin drew his gun. But before he surrendered it to Jim, he squeezed its handle, and a small slim gleaming box dropped out.

"What was that?" Jim asked.

"Power unit. Gun's useless without it. You don't think I'd let you kill me, do you?"

Jim had to laugh. "I didn't have any plans for shooting you, Colin."

"Man has to be careful!"

"I suppose he does," Jim agreed. He studied the gun. It was a neatly made thing, hardly bigger than the palm of his hand, sleek and tapering. A trigger stud jutted from the butt. It looked like a useful weapon, Jim thought, something that the New Yorkers had missed all along. They were armed with knives and hatchets, and with power torches, but with nothing in between. And a power torch was an inconveniently imprecise weapon, good for blasting holes in a thick icecap, or for wiping out a horde of attacking wolves, but not so useful if you merely wanted to wound an enemy, or if you were killing for food. A good square-on jolt from a power torch didn't leave much left over to be eaten.

"Want to see how it works?" Colin asked.

"I'd like to."

"Come on with me, then, while this boring talk is going on. We'll find something and I'll shoot it for you. Come on!"

171

Jim was the uneasy one now. His father and Ted were in that tent with the Londoner officers, and no telling what the parley was all about. That left just three of them to keep an eye on all these Londoners—and now one of them was trying to lure him away from the group.

But the way to conquer distrust, Jim decided, was not by meeting it with distrust of one's own. By showing good faith he might win over at least one of these strangely unfriendly men.

"All right," he said. "Let's go."

He told Carl and Dave where he was going, and walked off across the ice with Colin. They struck out in a northerly direction, and soon they had gone a fair distance from the camping ground. The snow was uneven here, humped into low hillocks eight or ten feet high, and Jim realized unhappily that he was no longer in sight of the others.

Colin, though, did not seem particularly menacing. The Londoner still spouted questions in an endless stream, hardly pausing to digest one fact before he demanded another.

"How many people do you have in New York?"

"Eight hundred thousand."

"We have nine hundred thousand. What's the name of your Mayor?"

"Hawkes," Jim said. "He's a very old man."

"Aren't they all? Our Lord Mayor is a hundred years old. Is yours as old as that?"

"Not quite," Jim said. He grinned. "But he's getting there, though."

"Is there still a President of the United States?" Colin asked next.

"Not that I know of," Jim said. "We haven't

172

heard in a long while. The Presidents used to live in Washington. We haven't had contact with Washington."

"We have a king," Colin said. "He lives with us in London. But he doesn't do anything. The Lord Mayor rules. And Parliament. Do you have a Parliament? I mean, a Congress. Isn't that what it's called?"

"We just have a City Council," Jim said.

"What kind of city is New York? I thought it was supposed to be important. Why isn't there a President? Why no Congress?"

"We weren't the capital of the United States," Jim pointed out. "We were just the biggest city. But London was England's capital. So you've still got a king and a Parliament."

"We have a new king," Colin said. "Henry the Twelfth. His father died last year. That was King Charles the Fourth. Do you know anything about English history?"

"Some," Jim said. "My father's a historian. He's mostly interested in American history, but—"

"Do you know about Queen Elizabeth I?" Colin demanded. "Henry the Eighth? Richard the Third? Do you know how America was founded? We founded New York, you know."

"That's not true. The Dutch did."

"No, we did," Colin insisted. "We once owned all the United States. And then we set them free, in 1776. That was before the ice came, you understand. King George the Third didn't like you Americans, and he said he wouldn't rule you any more, that you have to take care of yourselves from now on. So—"

"You've got it upside down," Jim said. "We were the ones who got rid of King George. The Revolutionary War—"

"Don't tell me," Colin broke in. "Just because I'm a soldier, I'm not ignorant! I can read, do you know that? I can read, and I've read the history books! We owned you, your whole country, and then we said, 'Poof, be free,' and you were free! That's how mighty we were then! And also—"

Jim had to fight off laughter. Colin chattered on, words pouring from him, misinformation piled on misinformation. Jim wanted to grab hold of him and shake him and say, "No, that's not how it happened at all. My father's a historian, and he can tell you the truth about these things." But what was the use? Colin was firmly in possession of his own view of history, and no quick argument was going to sway him.

"And then your George Washington came to London," Colin was saying, "and thanked our King George for letting the Americans go free, and—"

He cut his history lesson short and pointed.

"Look!" he cried. "There's a moose! Come with me! I'll show you how this gun works, now!"

The huge creature had wandered unsuspectingly toward them. Now, pausing, it looked up, its dull eyes blinking, its drooping snout twitching suspiciously. It was a spectacular beast, towering nine or ten feet, its forest of antlers gnarled and contorted. For a moment, it did not react at all as Colin ran toward it. Danger signals were filtering through its slow brain, but it had not yet come to a decision to flee.

Colin was within twenty yards of it now, Jim

174

following close behind. Jim watched the Londoner extend his arm, take aim, nudge the trigger.

There was a loud splat of sound. The moose snorted and reared high, its hoofs clawing at the sky in pain. A blossom of bright red sprouted high along its withers.

Colin muttered something in irritation. He fired a second time, and drew a crease along the huge creature's back, again not wounding it seriously. The moose whirled, sounded its trumpeting cry of anguish and fury, and rumbled into action. It began to run.

But not to flee.

Unexpectedly, astonishingly, the moose wheeled and charged, running with all its speed straight at its tormentor!

# 14

## Treachery

COLIN HAD NO CHANCE TO MOVE. HE STOOD AS THOUGH frozen to the ice while the giant moose bore down on him.

"*Colin!*" Jim yelled.

The Londoner finally reacted, in time to save himself though not in time to avoid injury entirely. He leaped to one side just as the enraged animal thundered through the place where he had been standing. The flank of the beast caught Colin and he fell heavily to the ice. His gun went skittering twenty feet away.

He lay there, stunned. The moose had reversed itself and was coming back, now, determined to trample him. Jim scrambled across the ice toward the gun. In order to reach it, he had to get between Colin and the moose, and that was no pleasure.

Moving fast, he threw himself headlong, slid across the ice, clapped his hand down on the gun. The moose came roaring past him, the sharp hoofs pounding down only inches from where he lay. He raised the gun and fired in almost the same motion. Luck guided his aim. The shot smashed into the moose's left foreleg, halting the creature in full career. It stumbled as the useless leg crumpled beneath it, and crashed heavily to the ice no more than five feet from Colin.

Getting to his feet, Jim fired again. This shot ripped through the moose's brain. There was a thrashing of legs for a moment, and then no motion. Panting, Jim lowered the gun, looked over at Colin.

The Londoner boy was getting shakily to his feet. He walked around the moose, looking at it in awe.

"Close one," he said.

"Are you all right?"

Colin rubbed his side. "I'll look a little purple tonight. But I'm all right, I guess. In better shape than *he* is, at any rate!"

"Here," Jim said, handing Colin back his gun. "Next time bring him down on the first shot. It's safer that way."

Colin holstered the weapon and stared strangely at Jim. "You saved me," he said. "You ran right in front of the big fellow to pick up the gun! You could have been killed, but you saved me. Why did you do that?"

Of all Colin's many questions, this was the most baffling. "Why?" Jim repeated. "*Why*? Well—don't you see—I couldn't have just let you be trampled, could I?"

"Why not? What am I to you? Am I worth losing your life for?"

"Stop talking foolishness," Jim snapped. "I didn't stop to consider the possibilities. The moose was charging you and I had a chance to get the gun and kill him, that's all. You make it sound as though I were a fool to have saved you."

"Maybe you were," Colin said in an odd, strained voice.

"Forget it, will you? We'd better go back and get some help to drag this animal. He's too big for the two of us. We can have a feast tonight—to celebrate the meeting between Londoners and New Yorkers."

They started to walk back toward the camp. Colin was silent, lost in some private meditation. Lines of tension stood out on his face, and Jim saw him chewing his lip with painful intensity. After a moment Colin said, "I guess I ought to tell you."

"Tell me what?"

"You saved my life. I've got to tell you."

"Will you say it then, man? What's the mystery all about?"

Colin looked down at his boots. "There isn't going to be any feast tonight. At least, if there is, you five aren't going to be at it. We're supposed to kill you."

"*What?*"

Colin blurted the words in panicky urgency. "You people are supposed to be invaders. We don't trust you. London doesn't, that is. The Lord Mayor thinks you're just an advance unit of a full-scale invasion. You want our atomic power plant, they

178

say. Your own must be running down, and so you're coming to get ours, for why else would people cross thousands of miles? So we were sent out to meet you. We were instructed to learn all we could from you—and then wipe you out!"

"No!"

"It's the truth!" Colin moaned. "We have to capture your equipment and bring it back."

"This is insanity! We came out of friendship. There's no invasion. London is invasion-crazy."

Shrugging, Colin said, "I'm sorry. Those were our orders."

Jim stared in disbelief. Then, from far off, came the sound of shouting—and a series of reports that might very well have been shots from Londoner guns. Jim gasped. His father, Ted, Carl, Dave —only four of them, against dozens of the Londoners! It would be a massacre! And what help could he be, more than a mile away, armed only with a knife?

"It's starting," Colin whispered.

"Come on, then. I've got to get back."

"You'll be killed, too!"

"At least I'll die fighting," Jim said. He drew his knife, hefted it a moment, then suddenly lunged at Colin. He locked one arm around Colin's shoulders and held the point of the knife at the Londoner's throat.

"Easy, man!" Colin said hoarsely. "First you save me, now you threaten me?"

"I want your gun. I can't go back there unarmed."

"Take it, then. It was yours for the asking! Do you think I'm still an enemy, Jim?"

"From now on," Jim said darkly, "everyone's an

enemy until I know otherwise." He snatched the gun from Colin's holster and gripped it tight, welcoming its reassuring sleekness against his palm. For a moment, Jim debated killing Colin on the spot. He was, after all, a member of the Londoner army. But he realized he could not do it, not this way, in cold blood. Colin had given him warning, hadn't he? Which side was Colin now on?

Even Colin didn't seem sure of that. Jim let go of him, and the Londoner stood like a sleepwalker, brow furrowed, head shaking slowly from side to side.

"Here," Jim said. "Take this!"

He tossed his knife down at Colin's feet. Then, without waiting for the Londoner to follow, Jim turned and raced off, back toward the place where the two parties had met.

He could see the fighting long before he reached the camp. It was hard to tell exactly what was happening, but flames were rising, and the tent where his father and Ted had been conferring with Moncrieff was a blazing ruin. Tiny sticklike figures were huddled in the snow, and now and then a burst of light from a power torch would flare out from the westward sleds.

Coming closer, Jim could make out something of the battle. His own people were dug in behind the sleds. The Londoners had scattered in a wide arc, and were sniping with their guns. Jim looked down at the gun in his hand, and wondered how long it would fire without running down. If he could slip around unnoticed behind the Londoner sleds, and pick them off from the rear without getting ashed by a New Yorker power torch in error . . .

No, he thought dismally. Fighting, killing, that wasn't the answer. It never was.

"We've got to stop them," Colin whispered, coming up alongside Jim. "It's insanity!"

"You think so, too?"

"Of course I do! They'll never get anywhere this way. Look, they've got some of your people prisoner already."

Jim stared. Yes, Colin was right! There, far behind the line of battle, a Londoner held Dr. Barnes and Ted Callison at gunpoint. So only Carl and Dave were still at liberty, holding their own behind the barricade of the sleds. Two men against a whole squad!

"Listen to me," Colin said urgently. "We've got to go out there and stop them. I don't know how, but we've got to do it!"

"Agreed." Jim pointed toward the scene of the fighting. "You talk to Moncrieff. I'll try to slip around behind those sleds to my own side. If we can only get them to stop shooting at each other, we can come to an understanding."

Colin nodded. He and Jim split up, and began to circle warily toward their respective lines. Jim moved in a half crouch, trying to look in every direction at once, hoping that Carl or Dave would recognize him and not just blaze away.

He had not gone more than a few steps when a Londoner rose out of nowhere, taking Jim off guard. He was young, and his hair was so blond it seemed almost white. One side of his face was singed; evidently he had come perilously close to a power-torch blast. His uniform was burned away on that side, too. But he held a gun in his other hand, and he was taking dead aim.

181

A figure suddenly cut between Jim and the Londoner.

Colin.

"Wait!" Colin cried. "Don't shoot him!"

The Londoner gestured with his gun. "Get out of the way, Colin! Have you lost your mind?"

"Don't shoot him!" Colin repeated. And suddenly Jim's knife flashed bright in Colin's hand.

Jim stared. The Londoner, apparently unable to believe that one of his own comrades would attack him, brushed Colin angrily out of the way and took aim at Jim. But Colin swiped with the knife. The blond Londoner howled. His gun went off, a wild shot, as Colin's blade sliced into the man's arm. The Londoner fell to the ground, clasping a hand to his wound. Colin stooped, picked up the gun, and stood staring at it strangely, as though he had never seen such a thing before.

Then he snapped out of his brooding reverie. He grinned at Jim, and sprinted off toward his own line.

Jim crouched again, began once again to circle behind the sleds. As he came around parallel to them, he caught sight of Carl and Dave, dug in solidly, power torches at the ready. Carl saw him and whirled, lifting his torch.

Jim threw up his hands. "Don't! It's me! Jim!"

Carl looked baffled for a moment. He gestured to Jim, who threw himself to the ground and crawled twenty yards over open ice to the safety of the sleds. Bullets whined past him, but did no harm.

Carl said, "You picked a sweet time to wander off!"

"How was I to know? What happened?"

"Your father and Ted were parleying in the tent. The talk went on and on. Suddenly Ted and Dr. Barnes came rushing out, but Londoner soldiers surrounded them. We realized they were being captured, so we scuttled back behind the sleds. Next thing we knew, the Londoners were opening fire on us. And here we are. Three of us against a whole mob."

"We don't stand a chance," Jim said.

"At least we'll go down fighting," Dave said, aiming his torch and firing.

"Don't be a fool," Jim snapped. "We aren't any good to anybody dead, are we?"

"What do you suggest?" Carl asked.

"Throw down your torches. Surrender."

Dave gasped. "Are you out of your mind? They'll kill us!"

"I don't think so," Jim said. "They've got the wrong ideas about us. They think we're the vanguard of an invading army. I talked to one of their men. He's going to get Moncrieff to call off the shooting. He'll tell them how few we really are."

"Can you trust any of them?" Dave asked. "After the trick they pulled just now?"

"We've *got* to trust them," Jim said passionately. "It's either that or be killed out there."

"Or kill them," Carl said.

"What good is that?" Jim asked.

"At least we'll still be alive."

It took some hard convincing, but Jim got Carl and Dave to see that there was nothing to gain and everything to lose by continuing to fight. They were outnumbered, and they could only trust to Colin's luck in persuading Moncrieff to call off the attack.

"Truce!" Jim yelled. "I call for truce!"

"Throw down your weapons!" came the Londoner reply.

"Go on," Jim whispered.

Carl and Dave hesitated. Then, with obvious reluctance, they tossed their power torches out in front of the sleds. Jim threw the gun he had taken from Colin down next to them. All three New Yorkers stepped forward, moving slowly into the open. Jim had never felt more exposed in his life. Suppose Colin hadn't persuaded Moncrieff? Suppose the Londoners were still intent on wiping them out?

The haze cleared. The smoke of battle rose and was gone. It was terribly quiet now. Londoners rose from their hiding places in the snow, shading their eyes to stare at the advancing New Yorkers. The battle was over.

It had all been so unnecessary, Jim thought. They had come in peace. They had meant no harm. They had only wanted to join hands across the frozen sea. And to be met this way, with guns, with deceit . . .

Moncrieff was coming forward. Two soldiers were leading Dr. Barnes and Ted. The Londoners were still armed.

"We called for truce," Jim said quietly. "We threw down our weapons. You should do the same."

Moncrieff shrugged. His eyes were sad, he looked troubled, but the Londoner leader still seemed steely and arrogant. He gave a signal, and the five New Yorkers were herded together. This was no truce, Jim realized. They were prisoners.

Moncrieff said, "I had orders to kill all of you. We think you are spies. I could still kill you."

"Will you feel safer if you do?" Jim asked. "There are only five of us. We don't have weapons. We aren't an army. We're exiles from our own city."

"Perhaps so," Moncrieff said. "But am I to trust you? How can I know? It's safer to remove you."

Jim kicked at the snow angrily. "Where does trust begin? Are we all enemies, every man in the world? Isn't there any way to break out of the trap of suspicion?"

Moncrieff's icy expression seemed to soften. "Perhaps," he said in a low voice. "But there are so many dangers. We have to move slowly, cautiously. We—"

He stopped and looked upward in surprise.

There was a sudden strange sound in the sky.

It was like no sound Jim had ever heard before. It was a dull rumbling that grew louder and more terrifying with each second, until it seemed that the heavens would split asunder. It swelled into a fierce roaring whine, a high-pitched screech that made eardrums protest and sweat run cold. No animal could make such a sound, Jim thought. No animal ever spawned could emit such an earjarring racket!

But what was it?

Londoners and New Yorkers looked toward the sky. What hovered there was even more frightening than that terrible sound.

It was golden, and it was huge. A great winged thing soared overhead, moving in slow, serene loops over the battlefield, glistening so brightly

185

that the eye was forced to look away after a moment. Bright as the sun the thing gleamed, and its swept-back wings remained rigid as it soared. Round and round and round again, high overhead, and then descending, coming within a few hundred feet of the ice, swooping past like some monstrous bird of prey.

But this was no bird, Jim knew. This was no cousin of the shrieking gulls he had seen at sea. What soared overhead now was the work of man.

An airplane! It had to be!

It was like something from a myth, come to life. Once, Jim knew, the sky had been full of planes, planes that could fly round the whole world in a quarter of a day. So the books said. But one who finds the open sky itself a hard-to-imagine concept does not easily accept the idea of vehicles that can fly in the sky, superbly confident that the thin air will support them. This trip had been full of wonders for Jim, but none of the others, not the sight of the open sea itself, had moved him the way the soaring plane did.

A hush had fallen over the ice field. Jim saw that Colin was on his knees, silently mouthing prayers with fierce energy. Everyone gaped in awe at the thing in the sky.

The plane circled once more.

Then it was gone. A whine, a rumble in the distance—and silence.

Colin still stared at the sky. "What was it?" he whispered. "What could it have been?"

"How would I know?" a Londoner next to him said.

Jim glanced at his father, at Ted, at the others. "It was an airplane, wasn't it?"

186

Dr. Barnes nodded. "But where could it have come from?"

"Not from any of the underground cities," Ted said. "Underground cities don't have planes. So it must have come from the warm countries. A scout, probably. Looking for signs of life up here."

"A spy?" Jim asked.

"Yes," Colin said. "A spy!" He came up to Moncrieff, reached out to catch his leader's arm. "Don't you see, sir? It's a spy from the cities of the South. They're surveying us. They must be getting ready to invade us. We've got to tell London! It isn't these New Yorkers we should have worried about at all. It's the ones from the South, the ones with the planes!"

Moncrieff was silent a moment. His jaw muscles worked, knotting in his cheeks. Then he said, "You're right, Colin. You must be. This fighting is foolishness. That's the real danger, up there!" He looked at the five New Yorkers. "We've got to warn London. Will you come with us? We'll go to London together."

_____ **15**

## _"Bring Us No Spies!"_

THE BATTLE WAS OVER. THOSE WHO HAD BEEN BITTER enemies only minutes before now joined, and prepared to leave together. The Londoners seemed mute with a common shame. They felt the guilt of their treachery now—not theirs, really, but their leaders'. Yet they had fought, had nearly taken the lives of five innocent men, for no reason other than blind fear of strangers.

They boarded the sleds and glided eastward in silence, past the moose Jim had slain, and onward without stopping. The Londoner sleds led the way; Colin had joined the New Yorker party to serve as guide in case they became separated from the others. He rode with Jim and Ted in one of the New York sleds; Dr. Barnes, Carl, and Dave occupied the other one.

An hour of travel had passed, and the shadows of night were beginning to close in, when a second plane flew over them. This one did not stay to circle. It became audible in the distance, the by-now familiar rumble turning into a whine as the plane came nearer, and then the plane was there, a slim gleaming shape in the sky, and it seemed to hesitate for a moment, studying them, and then it was gone.

Soon after, the party halted for the night. Jim followed Colin into the group of Londoners and found them crouched around their radio. "Moncrieff's telling London about the planes," one of the Londoners explained.

Jim listened. Through the sputter of static came voices. Moncrieff cut in, telling the story in short, clipped sentences. Jim listened, sadly amused by it all. The Londoners at the far end kept interrupting with tense, worried questions. They seemed to see invaders on every side! If not the New Yorkers, then the senders of these mysterious planes. Why were they so suspicious, Jim wondered? Why not hope to make contact with the flying people, why not greet them in warmth?

No. There was something about living under the ground that changed a man's soul, Jim thought. You hid, cowering, from the air, from the sun and the sky and the clouds and the rain and the snow, and fright crept into your bones, so that you saw enemies on all fronts. Fear obsessed you. These

189

Londoners were sick with fear. New York had been no better. Hide! Bar the doors, block up the tunnels! Beware the unknown!

Well, at least the Londoners had some reason, he admitted. They *had* been invaded by barbarians, by the fur-clad folk of the ice-world, who somehow must have found the entrance to the London tunnel. Perhaps the London entrance was closer to the surface than New York's. But that had been thirty years ago. It was not astonishing that the hungry ones of the glacier would want to enter the warm fastness below the ice. But why assume that men of another city—just as comfortable as London, certainly—were invaders? Above all, Jim wondered, why think that these city folk of the South, powerful and wealthy, would want to invade London? No doubt the airplane people meant well, since London had nothing to offer them. But here were Colin's people, safe in their warm city, crazed with fear that the planes were the vanguard of an invasion.

"Stay away!" crackled the voice out of the radio. "Don't come back to London!"

Colin and Jim exchanged glances. "They can't mean that," Colin said.

Moncrieff went on speaking, his voice remaining level and measured. He pointed out the absurdity of sending a picked group of soldiers to the outer world and then refusing them admittance when they came back with word of danger. But the Londoner at the other end sounded almost hysterical.

"Stay away!" he chattered. "Bring us no spies! If you come, you'll lead the airplanes to us! We're sealing the tunnel. We want no invaders! Stay away! That's an order. *Stay away!"*

Moncrieff let out his breath in a long irritated sigh. "May I speak to the Lord Mayor?" he asked. "This is a wholly unreasonable attitude, and I must appeal to higher authority."

Much as he had loathed Moncrieff before, Jim had to admire the man now. His earlier treachery had been only a soldier's performance of duty. His orders had been to wipe out the invaders. And now, in the calm, stern way that he was reasoning with the panicky people in the underground city, he was showing great strength and determination.

But he seemed to be getting nowhere.

"They don't want us," Colin whispered in disbelief. "They're telling us to keep away! We can die out here in the snow, and they won't care!"

Jim heard the voice from the speaker: "You can't come here. Don't even try to call us. Radio contact might lead them to us. I order you to keep away and make no attempt at contact!"

"I insist on speaking with the Lord Mayor!" Moncrieff snapped. "This is a maximum security matter. Do you dare to take the responsibility of forbidding me to speak with him?"

Jim shook his head. "They're insane! Condemning their own men to death—out of fear!"

"It isn't right," Colin muttered. "They sent us out here to protect them, didn't they? And now they won't let us back. We didn't deserve that of them."

"Wait," a Londoner near the speaker said. "He's getting through! It's the Lord Mayor himself!"

A new voice could be heard now, clear and

strong above the static. Once again, Moncrieff went through the story—how the "invasion party" from New York had proved harmless, how mysterious scout-planes from who knew where had come by to investigate. There was no comment from the Lord Mayor. Jim wondered if the radio had gone dead. But then came a reply, at last.

Moncrieff looked up. A grin crossed his flinty face. "The Lord Mayor says we can come back. There's an end to this nonsense. They'll have the tunnel open for us. And for you New Yorkers, too."

Onward to London!

It was heartening to see that not all Londoners were hopelessly trapped in fear. That had been an awkward impasse, for a while. Where would they have gone, if London had refused to let them in? Not back to New York, surely. They would have been men without a city, condemned endlessly to roam the ice-world.

In the morning, they set out. Cold weather closed in on them. London was still several days' journey away, and the sudden change in weather slowed them. The temperature began to fall, from the thirty-degree level where it had remained for some days, down into the twenties, then still lower. The nights were cold and crystal-clear, with the temperature frequently dipping well below zero. The numbing cold was like a great hand, holding them back from London's warmth. Through the long days they huddled in the sleds, bowed down to hide from the knife-edge sharpness of the wind, and at night they crowded together in the tattered tents to keep from freezing. When a lone moose wandered by, they slew it for its meat—the provisions were running low, and with the weather turning bad they might not reach London very soon.

And then it began to snow.

The snow started with a light sprinkling, powdery flakes coming down out of metallic gray sky. But the coming of night seemed to speed the fall, and by morning, three inches of snow covered the sleds. And still it fell.

"I thought spring was coming," Ted grumbled. "I thought the world was warming up!"

The snow went on falling. It was impossible to see more than a dozen yards in any direction. The convoy sleds kept together until late that afternoon, and then suddenly Jim, who was riding with Colin and Ted, realized that the other sleds were nowhere in sight.

"Stop!" he cried. "We've become separated!"

They halted, and hallooed for the other sleds. For half an hour or more they bellowed into the storm, until their voices were hoarse and their throats raw.

"They're gone," Jim said. "They could be anywhere at all."

"Maybe we'll find them when the snow stops," Colin said hopefully.

But the snow did not stop. It continued for the rest of that day, and on through the night. A foot and a half of fresh, soft new snow had piled upon the hard-packed surface of the glacier. The sled was having hard going. Drifts were sometimes ten feet high, piled by the furious wind, and several times, unable to see in the driving snow, they rode right into one of the drifts and had to dig themselves out.

The power accumulators of the sled reached bottom and gave out. There had been no sunshine for days, and the sled could go no farther until its source of energy returned. They stopped, and pitched the tent, and worked all night to keep from getting buried in the drifting snow. This was the Ice Age with a vengeance, Jim thought! They had had comparatively mild weather their whole journey, but now the angry weather gods were hurling their worst! Snow, snow, and more snow. Would they ever find their way to London? He wondered gloomily what had become of his father and Dave and Carl.

The snow stopped, finally, after three consecutive days. The world was white and clean and new-minted, but the sun did not appear, and the sled could not be charged. They waited. The last of their moose meat went, and still they waited, through one dark day and a second. There were no signs of the other sleds.

On the third day, when the sun remained still behind its cloud covering, Ted went out to hunt. An hour passed, without sign of him, and then a vagrant snowflake spiraled down, and then another.

"Storm coming up," Jim said.

"No," Colin answered. "Just snow blowing out of the drifts."

But it *was* a storm. In fifteen minutes, it was as thick as the last one.

"Why doesn't he come back?" Colin asked anxiously. "Surely he didn't let himself get lost!"

"No," Jim said. "That wouldn't be like Ted."

Jim fired the power torch into the air, and

shouted himself hoarse once again. No one appeared, and the snow redoubled its onslaught. Finally, discouraged, he sank down into the sled, his head in his hands. Chet, Dom, Roy—his father, Dave, Carl—now Ted, too! He was alone, except for his new Londoner companion. But for what? To be lost in these eternal snows?

"Hellooooo!" a voice called, far away.

"Hello!" Colin cried. "Here we are! Hello!"

Jim sprang to his feet. A figure appeared, moments later, struggling doggedly through the storm.

It was Ted. He stumbled into the sled, breathless, snow crusting his hair. He carried the body of a wildcat, lean and stringy, not enough meat on it for a single decent meal.

Ted grinned wearily. "Here's dinner—more or less."

Late that day the storm ended. In the morning, the sun rose for the first time in nearly a week, and they started the sled and continued onward.

The weather was better for half a day. Then came more snow, and they had to halt. Hunger bit at their bellies. There was no food left, and in the snow they dared not leave the sled to hunt. Unless some luckless animal blundered right across their path, they would go hungry.

Hungry they went. Gaunt and tired and weak, they brushed snow from their eyes, and hid under the tent, and prayed for the sky to clear and the sun to return. But a quiet realization came over them, one by one, as the day ebbed without a break in the snowfall.

"We aren't going to make it," Colin said.

"Don't say that!" Ted hissed.

"It's true. We'll die in the snow. We'll never get to London."

"It'll clear soon," Jim said, hollowly and without even convincing himself. "It *has* to!"

"And if it doesn't?" Colin asked.

Jim shrugged. "We'll be awfully hungry."

"We're awfully hungry now," Ted said. He managed a faint grin. For the first time he, too, admitted defeat, as he said tiredly, "Perhaps Colin's right. Perhaps this *is* the end of the line."

"You, too?" Jim asked.

"Be realistic," Ted said.

There was silence. Finally Jim nodded. The snow fell like a curtain now, stifling them. He said leadenly, "We came a long way, anyhow. We gave it a good try." When you had done your best, he thought, there was no shame in failure.

Neither of them answered him.

Time stole away. The snow ended for a while, and the sun glimmered, weak and feeble. They did not start the sled.

"Let the accumulator charge," Ted said.

But Jim knew that it was not a matter of the accumulator. It was *they* that had run down. They no longer had the strength to go on. "We've got to keep going," he said.

He started the sled, and guided it on an uncertain course, slowly, bumpingly through the drifting snow. Colin lay curled on the floor of the sled, asleep, while Ted lolled half awake, numb with cold, weak with hunger and fatigue. Jim drove for a mile. Then a kind of lassitude crept over him. He did not feel like bothering any more. He was cold and tired and hungry. Ted and Colin were both asleep, and he wanted to sleep, too. To curl up on a fleecy bed of snow, to close his aching eyes, to rest, to sleep . . .

He heard a sound in the stillness. A far-off rumbling sound, that grew in volume and rose in pitch, and became a high whine, like that of one of the planes they had seen earlier. Jim smiled. A plane, here? It could only be a dream. And therefore he must be already asleep, he told himself.

Only a dream. . . .

# 16

## *Golden Awakening*

JIM WOKE.

His eyes fluttered open, and he looked for the snow, and for the sled. But he was in a room like no room he had ever seen. Its lofty ceiling was far above his head. He was lying in a bed, soft and comfortable, in a large room whose green walls pulsed with gentle light. It was a long moment before he convinced himself that this was no dream.

Shakily he rose from the bed. His tattered, filthy journeying clothes had somehow been exchanged for a light robe of some smooth, free-flowing gray fabric that did not seem to crease at all.

Irridescent high lights gleamed in the robe; it seemed as though strands of gold were woven in it. He walked toward the window, and found that it gave onto a sort of terrace. Unquestionably, like a sleepwalker, Jim stepped out on the balcony—

And gripped its rail in mortal terror. Sudden dizziness took hold of him. Beads of sweat burst from his forehead. He looked down, down, an unbelievable distance. It was five hundred feet or more to the ground! He had never known a height like that, so sheer a drop.

Far below, tiny dots of color moved. Graceful cars of blue and gold and red, topped with plastic bubbles, raced along in the street. Buildings rose on every side—giant towers, mighty vaults of steel and plastic.

Gradually Jim calmed. The sky overhead was warm and bright, flecked with cottony clouds. There was no snow here. Only the city, stretching to the horizon, tower after massive tower. A graceful network of airy bridges hung like gossamer in the air, linking building to building far above street level.

And the city was shining.

That was the only way Jim could describe it. The sleek sides of the huge buildings gleamed brightly in the warm daylight. It seemed as though row upon row of mirrors, a thousand feet high, blinked back at him.

He stepped back into the room. As he did so, a panel in the wall opened, and a figure entered: a man of middle years, shorter than Jim, whose olive-toned face was partly hidden by a thick black beard.

"Good morning."

199

"Good—morning," Jim said falteringly.

"Are you wondering where you are? You are in Rio de Janeiro. Our scout planes found you and brought you here, seven days ago. I am Dr. Carvalho."

"Rio—? But you speak English?"

"Oh, yes, we know some languages here." Dr. Carvalho grinned. "You gave us a little difficulty. You were badly frostbitten, and we thought you might lose a few toes. But you are all right. You have slept while we thawed you out."

"There were two others with me," Jim said.

"They are doing well," Dr. Carvalho replied. "They awoke yesterday. Come," the doctor said. "Come see your friends. And our city."

Jim followed him through the panel in the wall. He found himself in a small rectangular enclosure whose luminescent walls were inlaid with tiles of a glowing violet substance.

"Down," Carvalho said, and the enclosure sank.

It glided downward giving no sensation that they were descending, drifted to a silent halt. A wall opened. They stepped out, into another room.

"So you're awake!" Colin said.

The Londoner was garbed in one of the loose robes, too. He looked rested, healthy. Ted stood behind him, grinning broadly. Looking past him, Jim had a better view of the street from this lower floor: he could see people, tanned, happy-faced people, wearing tunics like his. They were on a sliding walkway, five bright metal strips moving at different speeds. This city seemed miracle piled on miracle.

And yet Jim felt a stab of uneasiness.

"Why are we here?" he asked. "Why did you rescue us?"

Dr. Carvalho looked astonished. "We found you in the snow. We could not leave you to die."

"You don't pick everybody you see in the snow, do you?"

"You had a sled. You were obviously city people. We had to know who you were, where you were from. Your friends here have told us everything—how you came from New York, hoping to meet the Londoners, and how you were disappointed."

Jim whirled on Colin and Ted. "You shouldn't have opened your mouth! You shouldn't have said a word to them!"

Colin gasped. "Lord, and why not?"

"Who knows what they want?"

"We want only to be friendly," Carvalho said, his voice gentle. "Why are you so suspicious of us?"

Colin nodded. Almost playfully, he said, "You complained *I* was suspicious! And now here you are doing the same thing!"

Jim was startled. Then, as he realized how he must have seemed to the others, he began to laugh. It was contagious, then, this business of mistrust! He had fallen into the old trap, the automatic reflex of hostility that had caused so much trouble in the world.

Jim said, "There were other sleds in our party. We became separated from them in the snow."

"Yes. I know."

"Were—did you—were any of those other sleds seen?"

201

Carvalho nodded. "Yes. Our reconnaissance plane followed them to London. They reached London safely."

"Are you sure? All the sleds?"

"The whole party," Dr. Carvalho said. "They were never in danger. Your sled was the only one that went astray."

Jim let out a long sigh of relief. So his father was safe in London, then. And Dave, and Carl. And even Moncrieff and the Londoners. They had all made it. But Jim still looked troubled.

"What do you want with us?" he asked, a shade too belligerently.

Dr. Carvalho said gently, "You must not fear us, Jim. We of Brazil want only to help you and your people."

"You weren't much help three hundred years ago!"

The doctor looked pained. "For this, we feel great guilt. We turned our back on our responsibilities. But things are different now. The nations near the equator are making plans for aiding you of the north and south. We have much to atone for, and we have already begun. The ice is rolling back. Five, ten miles a year, now, but soon much more rapidly. The world will be reborn. And we must make it possible for your people to reclaim their heritage."

Jim shook his head. "It won't work. They don't want to come out of the ground. They *like* it down there."

Smiling, the Brazilian said, "They will change their minds. Only let someone go among them to tell them how sweet the air smells in spring, and they will come forth."

"They won't listen!" Jim insisted.

"We shall see." Carvalho let one hand rest on Jim's shoulder, the other on Colin's. "We will go to see them. You and Ted and Colin, and a boy from Brazil. Ambassadors from the world of warmth. There must be contact. Your party was the first to emerge. We have waited for someone to come from the underground cities, and now someone has. There is a stirring. Together, we will bring your people forth. The time is drawing near for the melting of the ice, and there is a great deal to be done. Will you help?"

Jim was silent a moment. Carvalho seemed to mean it, he thought. The old isolation of the warm-climate people was dead, then. There would no longer be guards along the borders. Thousands would pour forth from the underground cities —and the people of the warmer lands would stand ready to help the less fortunate ones rebuild their glacier-crushed nations.

Things were changing. With his father and Carl and Dave safe in London, as Carvalho had said, there would be the beginning of a new day of understanding in that city, at least. London had taken three strangers in. That meant London was loosening up, shedding its fear of change, of re-birth. The presence of three New Yorkers there would hurry that process along. Awakening New York might be a more difficult task, but it could be done.

They would do it.

He and Ted and Colin would go winging north-ward again in a gleaming ship of the air. First to London, to be reunited with the others, and that would be a day of jubilation! And then on—to New

203

York and all the other cities—ambasadors heralding the new day of warmth.

He walked to the window and looked out in wonder and awe at Rio's splendor—at the sun, the blue sky, the busy, healthy people, the stunning towers. Then he turned, and glanced at Ted and Colin, and at the Brazilian.

"Yes," Jim said. "There'll be a lot to do, won't there?"

It was like a dream. To awaken in this land of warmth after that nightmare of snow and ice . . .

But it was no dream. Rio was real, the warm sun overhead was real, Carvalho was real.

Soon the rays of that sun would lick at the ice that gripped half the world. Soon the grim glacier would fall back in defeat. A thaw was beginning —not only in the weather, but in the minds of men as well. Jim knew a great responsibility lay upon him now.

Carvalho said, "There are many who want to meet you three. We are full of questions about your cities. But not now. You will rest now, and rebuild your strength. Then there will be time for questions."

"I want to see the city," Jim said. "I want to walk in the street, with the sky over my head." He felt gay, giddy, unfettered at last. All somberness lay behind him.

And a mighty task lay ahead. It did not frighten him, though, the thought of rebuilding a world. What he had been through was discipline enough for any kind of job.

"There'll be so much to do," Ted said.

"Yes," Jim said. "Plenty to do. But it'll all be

worth doing. I can't wait to begin."

He looked toward the window—toward the golden light of the sun, the warming sun, the sun whose gentle rays would soon be driving back the ice, the sun that would give the world back to mankind.

# POUL ANDERSON
## Winner of 7 Hugos and 3 Nebulas

# PHILIP JOSÉ FARMER

## THE BEST IN SCIENCE FICTION